Beauty and the VAMPIRE

BOOK 1

DEMELZA BROWN
& EM BROWN

Beauty and the VAMPIRE

BOOK 1

Prologue

O nce upon a time there lived a nobleman, the Earl of Blackbourne. Handsome and charming, Blackbourne lived a life of luxury, coveted and wooed by many in polite society.

One fateful night, a young woman and her family, traveling across his land, required shelter from the storm. The earl seduced the young woman, but they were discovered by her mother, who demanded that Blackbourne offer to marry her compromised daughter.

Blackbourne refused, scoffing that the daughter had neither enough breeding nor beauty to merit his hand in marriage.

As the family departed, the mother put a

curse upon Blackbourne:

For your want of goodness and love
In body and soul shall you starve,
Forever suffer a thirst unquenched,
And burn in a lust un-doused.
Till you find your true beauty,
Shall you from your curse be free.

Chapter One

S omething was amiss.

Daliyah felt it the instant she awoke, her head having struck the side of the carriage that now jostled along a rough and brambled forest road between ghostly white birch trees and tall oaks that darkened the coming dusk as much as the rain clouds gathered above them. Her mistress, Miss Anne Cameron, sitting opposite her, and Emma, the other maid, had both stiffened upon hearing the howl of wolves. As had been described to them back at the posting inn, the wailing sounded beyond ordinary.

"You'll not want to go through Forest Blackbourne," Daliyah had overheard the grizzled innkeeper tell the carriage driver, Mr. Phillips. "Some as go in ain't been known to come out."

"How absurd," Miss Cameron had declared as she emerged from the private room where she had retired to rest while the horses were being changed. "You make it sound as if the forest were haunted."

A beauty of the first order with her golden locks, porcelain complexion, small mouth, and bright sapphire eyes, Miss Cameron never failed to command a level of awe.

The innkeeper bowed several times at her appearance, but his eyes had grown wide as if the mere mention of the supernatural might conjure forces unknown upon them. "Mayhap not haunted, m'lady, but cursed."

Miss Cameron had raised a perfectly manicured brow in disdain. "Cursed?"

"They say it be the Earl of Blackbourne, upon whose land the forest sits. He cursed the forest."

Miss Cameron had perked at the mention of a nobleman. "The Earl of Blackbourne?"

"The forest surrounds his castle."

"Is he there now?"

The innkeeper had shrugged. "No one knows, m'lady. I've not set eyes upon the man in several years. Only his manservant comes round the village."

"Perhaps he prefers residing in Town. In any case, I think he will understand our need to use the road through Forest Blackbourne, as I understand it will take thrice as long to go around it. We are delayed several days in our travels already, and I would prefer the most direct route."

The innkeeper frowned. Daliyah discerned true concern in his countenance and dismay in the manner in which he tugged and twisted the hem of his waistcoat.

"And wolves," the man said. "There be wolves, but not ordinary wolves, mind you."

Mr. Phillips, who seemed to share in his mistress' skepticism, remarked, "What do you mean by 'not ordinary wolves'?"

"You've but to listen to their bone-chilling howls to understand. Mr. Alders, a strapping young man, barely survived the forest with his life after being attacked by one. Said it was the largest and most ferocious monster he had ever come across."

"Ah, then people *have* emerged from Forest Blackbourne," Miss Cameron noted.

"Mr. Alders was not far in."

"I would be more wary of highwaymen than wolves," Mr. Phillips said to the innkeeper, "but myself and the footman have our firearms, and Jeremy is an excellent shot."

"Then spare not a minute more than necessary in readying the carriage," Miss Cameron said to him, "for I should like to be on our way."

One might not think her in great haste given how late she had risen from bed and how leisurely she had taken her breakfast each day. And of course her toilette required at least an hour's time. Daliyah would have wagered Miss Cameron to be among the most beautiful women in all of England, even were her golden curls not perfectly coiffed, the rouge not perfectly applied upon her alabaster complexion, and her corset not perfectly laced to accentuate her narrow waist.

However, they had been delayed several days in their journey primarily because Colonel James, a friend of Miss Cameron's father and who was to accompany her to London, had fallen ill midway in their travels. It was eventually determined that he could not continue, but Miss Cameron refused to turn back and insisted that she would press on despite the questionable wisdom of a young woman traveling on her own.

Daliyah understood that Miss Cameron, who'd had her come-out the year before, had decided that she would find a husband this year before her brothers ruined the family name. The elder Cameron brother was a profligate with a penchant for betting high on hazard, and the younger a known coward for abandoning his regiment when the French took St. John's, Newfoundland, during the last war.

Tasked with collecting food for the trip, Daliyah finished bundling the bread, meat pies, and apples that had been purchased from the innkeeper's wife. After she had placed the basket into the carriage, a dark-skinned youth of about three and ten years in age approached her.

"Care to purchase a talisman for your journey, miss?" he asked, holding up several objects carved from wood and stone.

"Did you make these yourself?" Daliyah asked of the different shapes: a cross, horseshoe, elephant, and clover.

"My grandfather taught me how 'afore his sight started to fail."

"I'm sorry to hear that. What is your name?"

"Noah."

Daliyah picked up the elephant. "These are lovely."

"I sell the elephant for half a crown, but you can have it for a bob less."

Daliyah smiled. As an indentured servant, she had very little money and saved as much as she could, for Mr. Cameron had said he would allow her to purchase the fifth and final year of her covenant for ten pounds. She needed two more pounds to secure her freedom.

But she pulled a shilling and sixpence from her coin purse and handed it to the boy.

"Thank you, miss," he said with a smile. "My grandpapa and I live not far from the forest edge should you desire to buy another."

"Just you and your grandfather?" she asked.

"Yes, miss."

"You've no master? You are...free?"

"My grandpapa was granted manumission. In truth, he found me when I was but a babe. He took me in and raised me."

"We are but passing through on our way to London, but I will remember you should we pass this way on our return."

"I should like to see you again, miss."

He had turned next to Emma, who promptly waved him away from her as if she might catch a disease from his nearness.

Looking out the carriage window, Daliyah saw mostly darkness save what was lighted by the lantern at the front of the carriage. A shadow darted between bushes, a few yards from the carriage. Daliyah could not shake the strange premonition stirring in her veins. She fiddled with the carved elephant.

"The posting inn we were at had rooms to let," Daliyah dared to remark, though her mistress had never welcomed her thoughts.

Miss Cameron narrowed her bright blue eyes. "You say this for what purpose?"

"If we should decide to turn back—"

"Turn back? That be utter foolishness, especially as Mr. Phillips was assured that, once we are through the forest, there will be another village, with plenty of inns."

The women all started upon hearing another wolf howl. This one sounded closer.

Though Emma, a young and slender maid of nine and ten, often shared her mistress' disdain for Daliyah, she expressed some concern at continuing through the forest. "Jeremy said the forest likely be full of highwaymen."

"*I* have more to fear from highwaymen than you," Miss Cameron replied. "*I* could be held for ransom. But both Mr. Phillips and Jeremy have their firearms."

Even armed, Daliyah wondered that they would prove sufficient defense if they came across a band of highwaymen. She had seen Mr. Phillips sneak in several long sips of ale back at the posting inn.

Miss Cameron, dressed in a fine wool coat, a modish plumed hat adorning soft flaxen curls, was right that she would have more to fear at the hands of highwaymen. They would not know that the Cameron family was not as flush in the purse as their outward trappings suggested.

In truth, it was not highwaymen whom Daliyah feared. But why, then, did coldness grip her heart? Daliyah pulled her cloak closer about herself.

The carriage slowed.

"Highwaymen!" Emma cried.

They grew silent, listening for a voice or exchange of fire. Instead, they heard... growling.

"What the devil..." they heard Mr. Phillips remark.

The horses grew skittish. Peering out the window, Daliyah saw the shadow of a creature move between the trees. And another. Their forms resembled wolves.

One of the horses gave a high-pitched neigh. A single gunshot was fired. Emma screamed. Mr. Phillips slapped the reins, and the carriage lurched forward as the horses went into a gallop. The shadows pursued.

Another gunshot sounded. Emma screamed again. Miss Cameron was nearly thrown from her seat when the carriage veered at a turn in the road.

"What is this madness?" Miss Cameron demanded with widened eyes as the horses continued to pull the carriage at full speed.

Several minutes passed before the horses finally slowed. Eventually, they stopped. Mr. Phillips knocked upon the door.

"Mr. Phillips," Miss Cameron addressed, "were we pursued by highwaymen?"

"No, madam, wolves," the man answered. "A whole pack of them. I've never known wolves to attack, but these looked fair possessed."

Miss Cameron shivered.

"One of the wolves went after the mare. Thought we could stop at the castle up that hill that I might tend to her."

They all looked to the hill, atop which sat a stone castle two stories high with a baronial facade and two circular towers. Though Daliyah had never seen castles till she had come to England nearly four years ago, she guessed that the one they beheld was at least two hundred years old, though parts of the structure, having larger French windows, appeared more modern.

"Let us hope they will receive us," Miss Cameron agreed.

By the gait of the horses, Daliyah could tell the mare limped. Glancing at Emma, she saw that the young maid still appeared right frightened. Miss Cameron, though a little shaken, had gathered herself and began tucking loose tendrils of her hair back into place.

They passed the gates at the bottom of the hill and made their way toward the castle. Daliyah drew in a long breath. Her heartbeat had settled back to a normal pace, but she hardly felt at ease. They might have escaped the wolves, but Daliyah could not rid herself of the feeling that worse was to come.

Chapter Two

From the window of his bedchamber upon the second floor, the Earl of Blackbourne observed his prey—there were five of them—walking from the carriage. His dual appetites stirred, causing heat to swirl in his loins and his mouth to salivate.

It had been a fortnight since Montague had fed, but with the arrival of this traveling party, he would not have to go into the village to hunt tonight.

How fortuitous.

Walking over to a tall looking glass, he assured his dark brown hair was neatly tied with a bow at the back of his neck. From his tall, wide brow to his disarming smile, there was not a part of him that did not enthrall, particularly among the gentle sex. He slid into an embroidered single-breasted coat, cut away to reveal his silk waistcoat and breeches that molded his form. Save for when he was hunting, he did not engage in sport as often as he once did, but one of the unexpected benefits of the curse was that he easily retained his strength and build.

After adjusting his cravat, he was ready to greet the party that had unwittingly walked into their deaths. Addison, the only servant remaining at Castle Blackbourne, had allowed them in. Montague could hear them in the foyer and could scent them the instant he stepped into the corridor outside his bedchamber.

Halfway across the expansive balcony at the top of the stairs, he stopped.

She was beautiful.

Long lashes fringed crystalline eyes of sapphire. A lovely blush graced high, soft cheekbones. She had a long and inviting neck, thin pink lips, a slender nose, and golden hair that shone even in the dim lighting of the castle.

He felt a tug at his groin, and his fangs

threatened to protrude. Taking a long breath to calm himself, he passed his tongue over his teeth to ensure they were at a normal length before proceeding down the wide staircase that spilled to the foyer.

"—should like to trespass upon the hospitality of—" the beauty was saying to Addison when she beheld Montague. All eyes turned upon him, including the gaze of the redheaded maid who was casting demure glances at Addison.

Accustomed to admiring gazes—they appeared like mice blinded by light—Montague continued down the staircase. His regal bearing seemed to have awed them into silence, for none said a word till Addison greeted him.

"My lord, one of their horses was bitten in the leg by a wolf. They hope to nurse the horse here."

"But of course," Montague replied. "Nasty beasts, wolves."

"I never come across ones with such aggression," the driver said.

"It would seem the wolves about here are cursed with the madness of rabid dogs. I would suggest you travel no farther at this hour and stay as my guests for the night at Castle Blackbourne."

"My lord, you are too kind," replied the beauty with a graceful curtsy.

"I could not in good conscience allow you to venture back into the forest to face the wolves. They do not appear as often during the day."

The driver shook his head, still in awe of the wolves they had encountered.

"My man, Addison, will assist your animals into the stable. We have plenty of rooms." He turned to the beauty. "Your maidservants can have a room beside yours."

"Again, I thank you for your kindness, but that will not be necessary. They shall be more than pleased to avail themselves of the same quarters as your maids."

"I keep no maids."

The beauty was taken aback.

"There is only myself here, and Addison is more than capable of tending to all my needs. I prefer to keep my maids in my townhome in London."

The beauty seemed satisfied by the explanation, perhaps assuming that he spent most of his time in Town. In truth, he had not been to the city in several years. Not since the curse.

"The servants' quarters will do," she said. "You are most generous to take us in. We would be at quite a loss had we not happened upon your place. Fortune has indeed been gracious to us."

Montague only returned a tight-lipped smile. He would not dispute how wrong she was.

Addison cleared his throat, saying, "I shall assist in unloading your effects."

Montague turned to the beauty. "I fear I shall have to introduce myself. I am Blackbourne, your humble servant."

Her eyes brightened and she returned a curtsy to his bow. "My lord, a pleasure to make your acquaintance. I am Miss Cameron. Anne Cameron."

"Perhaps my lady would take supper with me?"

Her blush deepened. "Thank you."

"As my servant, Mr. Brooke, will be busy, permit me to show you to your chambers."

The beauty turned to the redheaded maid. "Emma, you may come assist in my toilette."

"Yes, madam."

Montague offered his arm to Miss Cameron and led her up the stairs. Emma followed behind them while the others followed Addison.

"You have quite an imposing abode," Miss Cameron said. "From the size and number of windows, I take it the castle was built within the last century?"

Despite having been chased by wolves, the beauty seemed in good spirits.

"The initial castle was constructed precisely two hundred years ago in the year 1568," he replied. "My grandfather, the third Earl of Blackbourne, had the expansion built."

He lit a candelabra before leading her down a dark corridor. They walked past several full-sized portraits of all the earls before him.

"Is there a Countess of Blackbourne?" She tried to sound nonchalant in her query.

"The last Countess of Blackbourne was my mother," he answered, trying not to stare at the lovely expanse of her neck and where he knew he could find a vein.

"Do you not find it lonely with but your manservant to keep you company?"

"I enjoy the solitude."

"I suppose I should as well, for the activities

of the city can be tiring."

"Do you engage in a great many activities?"

"They never end! There are theaters, concerts, soirees, and balls at every turn, not to mention Vauxhall and Ranelagh Gardens. By the end of each Season, I am quite spent!"

"And you feel obligated to attend all these activities?"

"Perhaps a married woman can dispense with a few of them, but I had my come-out but a year ago. I have had few moments to spare in my schedule, I assure you!"

"Your destination must be one of some urgency for you to attempt traveling through Blackbourne Forest at this hour."

"I am to stay with my aunt. She means to introduce me to— Well, I was expected to arrive yesterday but have been severely delayed."

He opened the door to a room in the same wing as his own chambers but not too near. After lighting a few of the candelabras and wall sconces, he went to start a fire in the hearth.

"Pray, you need not trouble yourself," said Miss Cameron. "I can wait for your manservant to attend to the fireplace."

"It is no trouble," Montague assured her. "I

regret that you will find these chambers rather dusty. I was not expecting company."

"My maid, Daliyah, can tend to the room. As you have but the one servant, I pray you make use of mine. It is the least I can offer in exchange for your hospitality."

He inclined his head. "A most gracious offer."

The compliment pleased her, for she brightened with a smile. He imagined having her pair of lips wrapped about his stiff cock.

"And if there is anything you desire, Miss Cameron, I pray you will not hesitate to ask it of me."

The silence that followed seemed pregnant with possibilities. After he had started a fire, Miss Cameron's footman arrived with her portmanteau. Montague departed to allow her to change before supper.

"Shall you feed tonight?" Addison asked after he had seen to the other servants as well as the carriage and horses.

Montague, sitting in the dark of his chambers, watched the dancing flame of the candle Addison held. Addison was five years his junior and stood half a head taller. With soft auburn locks and a fine build, he would have made for a popular nobleman's son—perhaps even more sought after among the fair sex than Montague had been, for Addison possessed a gentleness that women found comforting.

"I think I must," Montague replied. "I have been a fortnight without feeding. I had thought to go hunting again, but the arrival of this party has saved me the trouble."

After a silent pause, Addison spoke. "Miss Cameron—there is not likely to be a woman more beautiful than her in all of England. Or beyond."

Montague made no reply.

"She could be the one," Addison continued. "The one to break the curse."

"Even if she were, I've not a bloody clue as to *how* it could be done," Montague grumbled. "You know as well as I that the bloody witch who cursed me left me no instructions."

"Perhaps you are to feed on her?"

"Perhaps. But what if that proves wrong? What if I cannot stop before I have consumed every last drop of her blood? I would, then, have killed my salvation."

Addison grew quiet in thought before saying, "I will review the books we have. We might have overlooked an answer."

Montague waved a dismissive hand. He would not stop Addison from poring over the texts they had amassed over the years, but for himself he found them a waste of time. Dozens of times over, he had read hundreds of accounts and references of the occult, of witches, sorcery, and curses. But it was difficult to discern truth from speculation, value from rubbish. The collection now sat in his library gathering dust.

"For certain, we must find a way to keep her here," Addison continued. "If you feel the need to feed—"

Montague laughed derisively. "If? You have been with me since the beginning. When have you known me not to be hungry for flesh and blood?"

"When you choose to feed, perhaps you should select the driver. He is her means of travel."

"It would be much more pleasurable to fuck one of the maids."

Montague was not above buggering a man when lust overpowered him, as it always did when he fed, but his natural preferences were for the fair sex.

"The maid, Emma, is pretty enough," he mused aloud. In truth, it little mattered how comely they were, feeling them thrashing beneath his body and hearing their desperate panting never failed to arouse. "But Miss Cameron is beyond lovely."

"You must not. Not before we have exhausted all hope—"

"Hope?" Montague echoed, disgusted by the word. "It has been several years, Addison, or have you lost count? The witch meant to curse me for the rest of time."

"But why would she have left you the words: till you find a true beauty, shall you from your curse be free?"

"To taunt me. To set me up for the harshest of disappointments. My God, I am so famished I could feed upon them all."

Addison frowned.

Montague rolled his eyes but capitulated, as he did from time to time when his younger half-brother reminded him of a sad puppy.

"Very well," Montague groused. "I will choose the driver first."

Satisfied, Addison departed to prepare the supper, leaving Montague to sit in the darkness once more. He steepled his fingers. For the first eighteen months, he had searched for the answer to his curse. There had been many women he thought might have been the one, but his hunger for their body and their blood had always prevailed. He despaired of ever breaking the curse.

Chapter Three

For the first time in a long time, Addison walked with lighter steps. He knew it was easier for him to retain hope. He was not the one who suffered from unholy appetites, though there had been times when he, too, had despaired of ever finding a cure. But he could not give up on Montague, a man who had been a brother and a father to him, who had saved his life by pulling him from the lake where he had nearly drowned at the age of seven.

As a child, Addison had worshipped Montague. When Addison grew more and more into the likeness of his father, the fourth Earl of Blackbourne had wanted to send Addison and his mother away. It was Montague, the sole heir to Blackbourne, who had convinced his father otherwise by threatening to enlist in His Majesty's Army to fight the French in the American colonies.

"Where is your driver, Mr. Phillips?" Addison asked of the Cameron footman as he entered the kitchen.

Jeremy, a young man with a rounded belly, thick arms, and a crooked nose that Addison suspected might have been broken at one time, replied as he sat down at the table, "Still tending the horses, I suspect."

"Do you think he requires assistance?"

Jeremy shrugged. As he showed no signs of peeling his arse off the chair, Addison grabbed a lantern and decided to see for himself. Outside, he found Mr. Phillips wrestling with the mare, who refused to be led into the stable despite the now steady fall of rain.

"What the bloody hell be the matter with you?" Mr. Phillips cursed, pulling at the reins.

Addison set down his lantern to assist. Mr. Phillips handed over the reins and swatted his crop at the horse. The creature neighed but still refused to budge.

"Perhaps we should dress her wounds first."

In surprise, the men turned around to see the darker of the maids standing near. She had said her name was Daliyah.

"In the blasted rain?" Mr. Phillips responded. "You be daft, woman."

Miss Daliyah approached the mare.

"Leave her be!" Mr. Phillips barked.

But Addison noticed the horse pawed the ground less. He held up his hand to silence the driver and watched curiously as the maid drew closer.

"I know your fear. I feel it too," she said in a calming tone to the mare.

Standing to the side of the horse, Miss Daliyah slowly lifted her hand and placed it upon its neck. Addison felt the reins relax. The horse stood still as the maid stroked her mane.

"You're hurt," Miss Daliyah said. "We ought dress your leg in the stables."

Feeling as if the horse might have understood the maid somehow, Addison handed the reins to Miss Daliyah, who began to lead the mare.

"Bah!" Mr. Phillips dismissed. "Blasted animal finally wants to be out of the rain."

Once the horse was situated in the stables, Addison looked more closely at the injured leg.

"One of the wolves tore her up good," Mr. Phillips said. "Might need a farrier to tell us if anything be broken."

Addison fetched bandages for Mr. Phillips, but when the man attempted to wrap the wound, the horse neighed and scampered away from him. Daliyah caught the reins and pulled the horse's head toward her. She put a calming hand upon the mare and spoke in gentle tones till the horse settled.

Impressed, Addison remarked, "You've a way with horses."

"She knows nothing of horses," Mr. Phillips said as he tended to the mare. "She be but a dressing maid."

Addison continued to look upon Miss Daliyah. With her long lashes, unblemished complexion, and soft contours of the face, she was rather comely.

"You must have worked with horses before," he said to her.

"I like animals," she replied, a vision of peace standing beside the horse.

Mr. Phillips snorted.

"And that is the extent of your experience?" Addison asked.

She nodded. When she met his gaze, he was struck by the luminosity of her eyes.

After Mr. Phillips was done, the mare allowed him to lead her into a stall.

"I would not have thought to believe the villagers when they said the forest was cursed," said Mr. Phillips, "but after our brush with them wolves, I wonder..."

Addison said nothing as he placed some hay before the mare, then climbed to the hayloft for more.

"We might have to engage a new team of horses," Mr. Phillips said. "Not likely the mare will want to be pushed hard with her injury."

"The nearest post is the one you came from," Addison informed.

Mr. Phillips scratched his gray hair. "Miss Cameron won't be too happy to go back."

"Is she in some haste to reach her destination?"

Mr. Phillips shrugged. "At times, yes. At times, no. There be no rhyme or reason to a woman's thinking."

After the horses had been seen to, they

prepared to return to the castle. Addison led the way, but after a few steps, Mr. Phillips stopped Daliyah.

"Listen here," he growled in a low voice. "I don't be needing assistance nor direction from your sort. The carriage and horses be my lot. You mind your own."

"Aye, sir," Miss Daliyah replied with her eyes downcast in deference.

When she resumed walking, Addison said to her, loud enough for Mr. Phillips to hear, "I neglected to thank you for your assistance, Miss Daliyah. If you had not come upon us, we might still be out in the rain struggling with the mare."

She made no reply and kept her head down. Upon returning to the castle and entering the kitchen, she was greeted irately by the other maid, Miss Emma.

"Daliyah! Where have you been? Miss Cameron desires her fichu, and since *you* packed her garments, it is best you retrieve it." Upon seeing the dirt and strands of hay upon the other maid's skirts, Miss Emma narrowed her eyes. "Miss Cameron will be none too pleased to have you serve her in such a state!"

Jeremy, who had not moved from where he sat, chortled.

"Fresh dirt ought to come off easy," Addison offered.

"Don't be long, Daliyah!" Emma admonished. "Miss Cameron is almost out of patience with you."

"Where can I find her chambers?" Miss Daliyah asked.

As if Miss Daliyah had made an inane query, Miss Emma sighed in exasperation. "The second floor. At the top of the stairs, turn left. It will be the first room on your right."

Daliyah hastened away.

Miss Emma turned to Addison. "Their kind, you understand, have not half our intelligence. It can be quite trying dealing with them."

Addison, having had few encounters to relate, could neither confirm nor contradict her statement. But he found himself curious to know more about Miss Daliyah.

Chapter Four

"Where have you been all this time?" Miss Cameron demanded when Daliyah entered the chambers of her mistress.

"I was attending the injured mare," Daliyah answered as she went into one of the chests to retrieve a fichu.

"And why would you do such a thing? That domain belongs to Mr. Phillips. You are a *maid* or had you forgotten?"

"I beg your pardon, mistress."

"I would rather you pay attention to your duties than offer apologies."

"Yes, mistress."

Miss Cameron eyed the fichu Daliyah held

out for her. "Are you stupid? That is not what I asked for. I wanted my silk shawl, the ivory one. It will pair well with my lavender gown. I intend to look my very best tonight when I dine with Lord Blackbourne. It is quite fortunate that we should have come across him in our time of need. He is certainly handsome. I am surprised there is no Countess of Blackbourne yet, but I suppose men like him must be particular in whom they choose to wed."

Daliyah listened quietly as she assisted Miss Cameron out of her traveling clothes and into her evening gown. While she agreed with Miss Cameron's assessment of Lord Blackbourne's physical assets, their host appealed none at all to Daliyah. There was something unnerving about the man, a chill that pervaded his air, except for a few brief moments when his eyes seemed to glow with lust. That would not have surprised Daliyah, given Miss Cameron's beauty, but he had gazed upon *all* of them in that manner.

"How do I look?" Miss Cameron asked when Daliyah had finished dressing her and redone her golden locks into a gentle coiffure.

Daliyah wondered that Miss Cameron posed

such a question as she surely knew there could be but one answer. "Lord Blackbourne must find you one of the loveliest women in all of England."

Reviewing herself in the mirror, Miss Cameron smiled and tugged on a ringlet that wound its way toward her decolletage. "I wonder that Lord Blackbourne does not keep more servants? I hope he is not low in the way of funds. Still, he is an *earl*."

Having finished with Miss Cameron, Daliyah made her way downstairs to the servants' quarters. Accustomed to sharing a room with other servants, she was surprised to find she had her own room.

Emma, who had a neighboring room, popped her head in. "Did you find Miss Cameron's fichu?"

"She wanted a shawl," Daliyah replied, wishing she had a shawl of her own. The castle felt even colder than the night air.

"Oh. I could have sworn she said she wanted her fichu."

Emma did not prevaricate convincingly, but there was nothing to be gained by pointing out her lie.

Daliyah unpacked a few things she would need for the night. She hoped they could leave as early as possible on the morrow. The unease in her stomach had doubled since setting foot inside Castle Blackbourne.

*****

As Daliyah stepped from her room, she came across Mr. Brooke holding several folded garments in his arms, which he held out to her.

"I found these petticoats," he said. "They might have belonged to the late Countess."

Daliyah did have a spare set of petticoats, though they were worn and in need of mending. The ones Mr. Brooke held looked to be in exceptional condition and even finer quality. "It is fair kind of you, sir, to lend—"

"Lend? I mean to gift them to you. They are of no use to myself or Lord Blackbourne."

She stared at the petticoats. They would be the finest she had ever owned. "Are you certain?" Had they no intention of ever hiring a maid?

"I am."

He gave her an encouraging smile, and she

accepted the generous bounty. The petticoats felt so soft in her hands, it was hard to imagine they belonged to a maid.

"I am much obliged to you, sir."

"I must admit I gift them to you with the hopes of currying your favor for a service."

"Offerings of any kind are unnecessary. How may I assist you?"

"As you have noticed, Lord Blackbourne keeps only myself for a servant. It would be hard for me to cook and attend his lordship's table at the same time. Would you be the serving maid for dinner tonight?"

"I am at your service, sir."

His countenance brightened and she was once again struck by his handsome features. He bowed. "I am most indebted to you, Miss Daliyah."

"Not at all, sir."

They walked together downstairs.

"What part of England do you hail from?" he asked.

"Miss Cameron is from Lincolnshire," she replied.

"I asked not of her but yourself."

She started. Few servants ever inquired

after her. "I hail more appropriately from Barbados. I came to England about four years ago."

"And how do you find England?"

He seemed genuinely interested in her answer.

"Well," she replied.

"You need not coat your answers with sugar to be polite. I take no offense if you find this country dreary and intolerable. I do."

She couldn't resist a soft chuckle. "I find there are aspects of England that are quite impressive."

"A most politic answer!" he accused with mock disapproval. "And I had thought I invited your honest opinion, Miss Daliyah."

"That is my honest opinion, sir."

"Then, pray tell, what aspects are *not* impressive to you?"

"The weather," she pronounced. "I am not accustomed to the cold. Though the heat in Barbados can sit upon you like a thick blanket, I prefer it to the chill."

As she spoke, she felt a cool tremor, though she found warmth in Mr. Brooke's affability.

"I should like to hear more of your thoughts

on England," he said before they parted ways, he to the kitchen and she to change out of her dirty petticoats.

"What are you doing with Miss Cameron's undergarments?" Emma asked as she passed Daliyah.

"Mr. Brooke gave me these," Daliyah answered.

As Daliyah predicted, Emma did not receive it well. "You mean you *stole* them."

"Not at all."

Emma's eyes widened and a pulse at her temple throbbed. "Why would Mr. Brooke—why would he give anything to *you*?"

"He noticed my petticoats were dirty."

Emma grabbed the petticoats. "You are mistaken. Nay, you are lying."

"I speak the truth," Daliyah responded, and tried to take the garments back from Emma.

But Emma held tight. "I mean to return to these Mr. Brooke. Miss Cameron will be quite upset to hear of your lies and theft!"

If she tried to pull the petticoats from Emma, they might tear, thus Daliyah relented. Despite her indignation, there was nothing to be gained by battling Emma. Forcing her lips together,

Daliyah left Emma, changed her petticoats, then went into the kitchen, where Mr. Brooke was busy cooking.

"I fear your mistress will be severely disappointed in her dinner," Mr. Brooke said. "I have never had to prepare a meal for anyone beyond myself and Lord Blackbourne."

Daliyah still found it strange that the earl did not employ more servants, especially a chef, but she had to suppose the earl, despite his title, was in difficult financial straits.

"We are grateful for your hospitality," Daliyah returned.

"When his lordship and your mistress have eaten, there will be bread and stew for the rest of you. Here is the first course for you to take up." He ladled soup into two bowls and set them on a tray for her. "When they are done, you can return to bring the next course. Wait—the bread."

He grabbed a bowl and then a basket of baked goods, but in his haste, spilled the rolls onto the table. Daliyah reached for one of the rolls at the same time as Mr. Brooke. His hand brushed hers. He paused. She could feel his gaze upon her and felt her cheeks grow warm.

"Your pardon," he said.

"How many rolls would you like to serve at dinner?" she asked, rattled that he had such an effect on her.

"All of them, as there are but four that have not been spilt upon the floor. I hope your mistress finds them passable. They are not fresh baked."

"We are grateful to be having dinner and not still stuck in the forest."

She carried the soup and bread upstairs to the dining hall. Despite the light from several candelabras and the fire burning brightly on the hearth, Daliyah found the room to have several areas of darkness, including the head of the table where Lord Blackbourne sat. He gazed upon Mistress Cameron with an intensity Daliyah found unnerving. It was the gaze of lust mixed with some other quality. Desperation, perhaps.

Nay, starvation.

His lordship straightened when Daliyah approached the table and set a bowl before Mistress Cameron. She wrinkled her nose.

"I fear you will find dinner plain and far below the standards you are accustomed to,"

Lord Blackbourne said. "At present, I have no cook in my employment."

Mistress Cameron's eyes widened. "No cook? Then who prepares your meals?"

"Mr. Brooke."

"Your manservant is your cook?"

"I require little in the way of fare," Lord Blackbourne said with a wryness Daliyah found peculiar.

Mistress Cameron continued to look perplexed. "Is it a hardship to employ a cook?"

Daliyah glanced at Lord Blackbourne to see if he took offense. A person of lesser beauty than Anne Cameron might be considered impudent for asking such a question.

"Not at all," his lordship replied, unperturbed. "I simply choose not to have such an expense. Mr. Brooke is all I need."

"How can—why only one servant?"

"Why house several servants when there is only me?"

Miss Cameron took a spoonful of the soup. "Mr. Brooke has some skill in cooking. The soup is not half bad. Have you always lived so frugally?"

At that, Lord Blackbourne shifted in his

chair and looked away for a moment. "No. But it is my preference now. I am a solitary man and capable of taking care of my own needs."

"That is an admirable trait. For myself, I cannot conceive of having fewer than half a dozen servants, at least, and if they are competent. But I suppose it must be easier for one of your sex to adjust than mine," Mistress Cameron concluded.

"Undoubtedly."

After Mistress Cameron finished, Daliyah took her bowl. She walked over to Lord Blackbourne and saw that his bowl was full. Had he not touched his soup at all?

He pushed the bowl toward her, indicating she should remove it. She set it on her tray and went downstairs to the kitchen where Mr. Brooke had prepared plates of stew and potatoes. Daliyah marveled that a single servant could manage such a large residence.

Back in the dining hall, Daliyah cast a few more furtive glances in the direction of Lord Blackbourne, who listened, patiently if not a little disinterested, to Mistress Cameron lament the unaccommodating road conditions, how she had tried to convince her father to replace their carriage with a newer, swifter vehicle, and how difficult it was to keep up with the latest ladies' fashions when they lived so far from London.

Blackbourne held a fork and moved his food around his plate but did not appear to actually eat.

Daliyah could not speak to why the man unnerved her when he had been nothing but hospitable in hosting all of them at his residence. He seemed to experience some difficulty as the dinner progressed, perhaps suffering from a stomach's ache, which would explain his lack of appetite. He kept his gaze averted from Mistress Cameron more and more.

"Do you plan to go into Town for the Season?" Mistress Cameron asked.

"I prefer the air of the country," he answered.

"As do I, but is there much to do in these parts? My father is partial to the country, but that is because his favorite pastime is hunting. But there is little in the way of entertainment for young women in the country unless there is a sizable assembly hall for dances. Do you plan on missing the entire Season?"

"I rarely leave Blackbourne."

Mistress Cameron blinked several times.

"Truly? When was the last time you were in Town?"

Blackbourne pressed his lips together. Daliyah wished she could communicate to her mistress that the present subject appeared to discomfort their host.

"Several years ago," he answered. "I am not partial to all the social obligations that should fall upon me when I am in Town."

"But then you miss all the gaiety! And social obligations need not be always bad. It depends upon the quality of your company. And though I quite understand how tiresome social calls must be, London has so much to offer that I should happily endure the miserable aspects to partake of the good."

"What do you favor when in Town?"

This allowed Mistress Cameron to launch into the dances, performances, gardens, and shops that she most looked forward to. She recounted almost every visit she had made to Vauxhall and its music, menagerie, and fireworks.

When Daliyah went to collect Lord Blackbourne's plate, whatever ailed him seemed to have worsened, for he gripped his fork till his knuckles turned white. His nostrils flared. For a moment, Daliyah sensed it was her nearness that discomfited him.

She took their plates downstairs. Lord Blackbourne's appeared as full as before.

"I fear dessert shall be a disappointment," Mr. Brooke said, looking upon a plate of biscuits.

Daliyah examined the simple squares of shortbread. "Perhaps we can serve it with a bit of jam?"

He brightened. "Aye, that will make it appear less plain."

"Your master ate very little," Daliyah said as she took the plates off her tray.

Mr. Brooke spoke with unconcern. "He doesn't eat—er, he often has a poor appetite."

She wondered what he could have meant to say at first, but Mr. Brooke undoubtedly wanted not to cast the earl as more peculiar than he already appeared. She took up the biscuits with tea. After serving her mistress, she approached Lord Blackbourne to pour his tea.

Clutching his napkin to his mouth as though he meant to retch, he leaped out of his chair.

"Forgive me," he said, still holding the

napkin to his mouth. "I just remembered something I have to attend. Please finish dinner without me."

With a quick bow, he strode out of the dining hall. Mistress Cameron stared after him with her mouth agape.

"What matter could have such urgency?" she wondered, then shook her head. "He is a most odd gentleman. A handsome one, but odd. Still, he is an earl, and I suppose they are entitled to their eccentricities. He really ought to take himself to Town. Being out here in the country can surely make a man mad."

Chapter Five

"You can sit yourself at the end there," Jeremy said to Daliyah, nodding toward the part of the table opposite from where he, Emma, and Mr. Phillips sat.

Her bowl of stew in hand, Daliyah sat apart from the others.

Mr. Brooke looked from her to the others, then took a seat opposite Daliyah.

"Mr. Brooke!" Emma cried. "That is quite unnecessary. She is accustomed to sitting on her own, I assure you."

"This is where I normally sit," Mr. Brooke replied cheerfully.

Emma looked at him with mouth agape.

Jeremy frowned and might have cast a more disapproving look if they did not all rely upon Mr. Brooke and Lord Blackbourne.

Daliyah stared into her bowl. She wanted to tell Mr. Brooke it would be best that he not sit near her, for Emma would only be upset and aim her vexation upon Daliyah at a later time.

"You must come sit with us," Emma tried.

"Thank you, I am well situated where I am," Mr. Brooke said as he spooned his stew.

"Your master keeps a strange house," Mr. Phillips commented. "How is it there are not other servants besides yourself?"

"Lord Blackbourne does not require a great deal of care."

"Do you fix all his meals?"

Mr. Brooke hesitated. "He often attends to those himself."

"The whole of the house rests upon your shoulders?" Emma asked.

"Lord Blackbourne uses few rooms. The rest of the rooms remain shuttered."

"I take it the servants' quarters be part of the original castle?" Mr. Phillips asked. "Feels uncommonly cold."

"Have you been in his employ long?" Emma

inquired. "He seems he could be quite the frightful man to work for." After Jeremy gave her an admonishing look, she added, "Though he is most gracious to host us for the night."

"I grew up in Castle Blackbourne," Mr. Brooke said with a little less cheer. He passed Daliyah the salt and explained, "Should you find the stew insufficiently flavorful."

Daliyah thanked him but wanted only to finish her meal so that she no longer had to be the target of Emma's glares.

"I hope we can trespass upon your hospitality in the morning," Mr. Phillips said, "and allow me the use of one of your horses to ride into town. I fear you may have to house the mare while she heals her injury."

"Of course, and if you are in no hurry, Lord Blackbourne has expressed that you may all stay at Castle Blackbourne."

"How kind!" Emma exclaimed.

"I know not how long the mare will require," Mr. Phillips remarked, "and if Mistress Cameron is comfortable with the arrangement, being as she is without a chaperone."

Mr. Brooke nodded. "We are at your service whatever your mistress decides."

Emma enthused, "How very fortunate we are to have come upon Blackbourne!"

At that, Mr. Brooke fixed his attention upon his food and said no more.

*****

"Did you know that Lord Blackbourne has extended his hospitality for as long as we shall need it?" Miss Cameron asked as Daliyah prepared her bed by sliding the warming pan beneath the bedclothes.

Miss Cameron's tone, suggesting that she was partial to accepting Lord Blackbourne's offer, struck some dread into Daliyah.

"Is he not a most generous man? I should accept without qualm, though I would that this castle were not nearly so cold." Miss Cameron wrapped a second shawl over her shoulders and moved to the fireplace, where Daliyah had begun hanging her night clothes to warm. "I have no place to stand if my garments take up the length of the hearth!"

Unable to quiet her dismay at staying longer at Castle Blackbourne, Daliyah asked, "Will not the delay dismay your aunt?"

It was wrong of her to ask, Daliyah knew, when Miss Cameron cast her an icy glare. "Of course I shall send word to my aunt that we are but temporarily delayed. I think she will be reassured to know that we are being hosted by an earl. She nearly married a baron once. The family had such high hopes, and it was such a disappointment that a marriage did not come to fruition. Can you imagine how everyone should react if I were to marry an *earl*?"

Daliyah kept her gaze lowered. While Lord Blackbourne was handsome, there was a quality about him that took the luster off his features. Daliyah understood it was the way of Miss Cameron's world to value the aristocracy, but she found no sound reason for such a practice.

"Come in," Miss Cameron responded to Emma's knock at the door.

"Are these petticoats yours, madam?" Emma asked after entering.

Daliyah frowned. "They were—"

But Miss Cameron silenced her with a look. She inspected the petticoats Emma held. "They are nice but not mine. Where did you come by them?"

Emma looked over at Daliyah. "She claims

Mr. Brooke gave them to her."

"He did!" Daliyah insisted. "You can ask him!"

"Foolish girl," Miss Cameron admonished. "Why would Mr. Brooke, a stranger to you, gift you such fine articles?"

"I worried she might have stolen your petticoats," Emma said.

"You must apologize at once to his lordship."

"I did not steal the petticoats!" Daliyah protested.

"Assist with my nightgown now. We must speak to Lord Blackbourne as soon as possible. I will not have him going to bed thinking I employ thieves."

Daliyah wondered that Miss Cameron would want to change into her nightgown *before* seeing Lord Blackbourne. A chaperone would surely balk at a young woman being seen by a man in such scant clothing.

Miss Cameron put only a shawl over her nightgown, then took the petticoats from Emma. "Come, Daliyah! I am beyond mortified."

"Miss Cameron, I vow that I speak the truth," Daliyah said as she followed her mistress down the corridor. "If you but ask Mr.

Brooke—"

"Silence!" Miss Cameron commanded. "I will hear no more lies from you."

As they neared the other wing of the castle, the chill grew more pronounced to Daliyah. They came upon Lord Blackbourne of a sudden in the corridor, as if he knew they were coming and had stepped out to meet them.

"Miss Cameron, I pray that all is well," he said.

He seemed to have recovered a little from what had ailed him during dinner. His gaze took in Miss Cameron from head to toe and came to rest upon the opening where the ties of Miss Cameron's shift had come undone. He seemed to miss nothing.

"I regret that it is not," Miss Cameron replied. "You have been naught but gracious and kind to take us in, and it greatly saddens and embarrasses me that one of my own maids should steal from you."

"I did not!" Daliyah pleaded. "Mr. Brooke gifted them to me."

Miss Cameron turned to her. "Apologize to his lordship."

Daliyah stared at her mistress as she

attempted to think how she could convince her otherwise.

She couldn't.

Turning to Lord Blackbourne, she relented. "Your pardon, my lord. I did not mean to take the petticoats."

"She hails from the West Indies," Miss Cameron explained to him. "They have a different upbringing there, and as she is an indentured servant, she has not the same incentives as paid servants. Please accept the return of your articles with my deepest, humblest apologies." She held out the petticoats. "I hope you will forgive this egregious trespass upon your hospitality?"

"Of course," Lord Blackbourne said. "In truth, I have no need for these petticoats. They might have been left here by a past guest. Please accept them as a gift from me."

"Oh! My lord, you are kindness itself!"

He bowed. "I pray you will all sleep well tonight."

Miss Cameron beamed. "How could we not? Good night, Lord Blackbourne, good night!"

He gave a small smile.

Daliyah knew not why, but she shivered.

Petticoats in hand, Miss Cameron returned to her own chambers and made straight for the fireplace. She handed the petticoats to Emma. "Take these. Lord Blackbourne has made a gift of them to me."

To Daliyah, she said, "My robe! I thought for certain I would catch a chill, though I think his lordship was charmed by my appearance. I had better not hear of you stealing anything else from here. And where is my milk tea? Have you forgotten I always have milk tea before bed?"

In the midst of the to-do concerning the petticoats, Daliyah *had* forgotten. She took her leave of Miss Cameron to fetch the milk tea.

As she turned the corner toward the staircase, a sudden movement in the shadows startled her, causing her to whirl around. She bumped into the banister and dropped her candle. The flame went out, leaving her in complete darkness. She did not fear the dark.

Until now.

She often preferred the quiet of night and found a certain peace to the dark. The glare of light brought those who would bark at her, shun her, and mistreat her.

But the darkness of Blackbourne had an

ominous quality. She stood where she was, unable to shake the tentacles of trepidation.

Before her light had gone out, she had thought she saw the form of Lord Blackbourne. Indeed, she thought she could make out his breathing. But why would he be walking the corridor sans a candle? And why would he be content to stand in the shadows?

She thought to address him, but in an instant, every nerve in her body stood at attention.

She sensed him standing *near* her. A cool air seemed to pass by the back of her neck.

"Daliyah!"

As quickly as it came, the presence left her.

Emma was rushing down the corridor. Coming upon Daliyah, she asked, "Why do you stand in the dark?"

"I dropped my candle," Daliyah replied and bent to pick it up.

Emma rolled her eyes and allowed Daliyah to light her candle with her own. "Miss Cameron wanted to remind you that she prefers her milk tea with sugar and not honey. You gave her honey the other night."

Daliyah had explained then that the posting

inn where they had stayed had run low on sugar, but it was of no use to offer the explanation a second time. She glanced around for Lord Blackbourne but saw no one. Perhaps she had been mistaken. After all, why would he be lurking in the dark?

"Don't dawdle or Miss Cameron will be more cross with you," Emma said.

Daliyah turned and made her way downstairs. After making the milk tea, she made certain to bring a tinderbox with her. She did not want to be without light in the darkness of Castle Blackbourne.

Chapter Six

Back in the anteroom of his bedchambers, Montague gripped the edge of a table till his knuckles turned white. It had taken all his forbearance not to reach out to the maid, wrap his fingers about her throat, and sink his teeth into her neck. To his surprise, her scent was particularly evocative, more mouthwatering than the finest cut of beefsteak, though he could hardly remember what it felt like to enjoy normal fare.

At the dinner table, every movement of hers had sent a wave of her aroma up his nose. Every part of his body had reacted, including—and perhaps especially—the area of his groin. It had churned with heat. Fortunately, the dining table had hid his stiffened member. Ever since the curse, his carnal desires and bloodlust were entwined as one.

He attributed his unusually strong reaction to the maid to the fact that he had not fed nor fucked in too long.

"You look unwell," Addison noted from the threshold after entering.

"I think I can hold my hunger at bay no longer," Montague replied. "Not when the temptations are so near, beneath mine own roof."

Addison looked down but nodded. He had long ago accepted the demon his brother had become. At first, neither of them had believed the curse. Montague had recently become the fifth Earl of Blackbourne. He had an income of fifteen thousand pounds per annum from his properties and a line of women willing to become the next Countess of Blackbourne. The world was his to command.

But that world had grown wretched in an instant.

He could not suppress the appetites that gnawed him from the inside. An evil spirit possessed him, overriding all faculties.

Succumbing one night, he had coaxed one of his own maids into bed and taken her.

Addison had discovered him the following morning, sitting in bed in shock, the blood of the maid dried upon his face, her crumpled body next to him.

He remembered the look of horror on Addison's face, how his brother had slumped to the ground and sat against the wall for what seemed like hours of silence before Montague instructed him to hide the maid's body. Addison had moved as if in a trance but obeyed.

After two more servants had disappeared, several of the remaining ones quit, believing the castle to be haunted, perhaps by the fourth Earl of Blackbourne. Addison had tried to stop Montague, but Montague was stronger. Once, Addison had resorted to locking his brother in the dungeon. For days, Montague had howled and roared, his cravings searing his body like a thousand pokers. He had tried to tear them out with his own hands and clawed at his flesh till he was red with blood. He had banged his head against the door.

Unable to endure his brother's agony any longer, Addison had relented.

Overcome with blinding thirst, Montague could have descended upon his own brother, but he happened to hear the approach of the rector in his gig, who came from time to time hoping to attract Montague into attending service. After he had finished with the clergyman, he'd found Addison beside the dungeon door, sobbing.

That was the day Montague ceased to believe in God.

"I think I shall avail myself of the maid," Montague said. "The one named Daliyah."

Addison looked up sharply. "I thought you had agreed to the driver, Mr. Phillips?"

Montague looked upon his brother in some surprise. Addison rarely cared whom Montague chose for a victim.

"Why would I choose old over young and a man over a woman?" Montague returned. "Not only would the young maid taste better, she would be a great deal more enjoyable to fuck."

"I don't care much for Mr. Phillips," Addison said. "And the maid be much finer on the eyes."

"If you wish to ravish her before I get to her, you have my permission."

"Well, I...I suspect the other maid more ready to lift her skirts."

"I feel as if I could feast upon them all tonight, such is the grandeur of my hunger."

"Mr. Phillips intends to return to the posting inn for a fresh set of horses in the morning. Once he secures them, there will be no reason for Miss Cameron to stay."

Montague eyed Addison. "You are keen that I choose him."

"One day less in his company would be agreeable. He has the room at the end of the servants' hall."

"They will all perish eventually." Though Addison surely knew this already, Montague felt oddly compelled to state the obvious.

"I know it," Addison said without flinching.

"Very well. I will take Mr. Phillips tonight, but if I am still famished after feeding upon him, I will have the maid next."

Chapter Seven

Daliyah lay upon her bed but could not sleep. The agitation from the attack of the wolves had yet to dissipate. Occasionally, she heard the howl of one of those frightening beasts. She trembled, though the sound came from a distance. Never before had she feared for her life, save when a severe storm threatened the ship that had taken her across the Atlantic to England. Even then, her apprehension had not sunk into her bones the way it had with the wolves. Did wolves even feast upon humans?

But the wolves were not the sole explanation for her restlessness. When faced being torn apart by the ferocious animals, she had welcomed the sight of Castle Blackbourne. But now that she was ensconced within its walls, she felt the opposite of safe. The castle exuded a disquiet that she could not shake. When she closed her eyes, she saw tortured souls.

The Earl of Blackbourne reflected his abode and its unease. Or perhaps the castle reflected *him*. The flare in his dark eyes when he had looked upon Miss Cameron was unsettling. Though many men could not tear their gazes from Miss Cameron, the intensity of the earl's suggested something beyond simple desires.

No one else, however, seemed unsettled by either the castle or Blackbourne himself.

In contrast, Mr. Brooke had a comforting presence and seemed a gentle soul. He would not be such a dedicated servant and have worked all these years at Castle Blackbourne if anything was amiss.

I am being silly and unnecessarily fearful.

With that thought, Daliyah closed her eyes and tried to sleep. She curled underneath the blanket as if the linen served as a protective layer against the malevolent air and wished she could close her ears to the sounds of the wind thrashing through the trees and the rain knocking at the small window near the ceiling of her room. There was grunting too. At first she thought Emma to be having a dream, but then realized there were two distinct voices: one that sounded like Emma, the other the lower pitch of a man.

The grunts were interspersed with gasps and the creaking of furniture. Daliyah flushed as she recognized the sounds of rutting.

"Oh, Mr. Brooke!" Emma gasped.

Turning to face the wall, Daliyah tried to ignore the sounds from the other room.

But they penetrated.

And stirred a warmth she seldom felt since her days when she had been in love with Isaiah. She remembered well the torrent of passion she had felt when he was near, how arousal flooded her body, urging her to join as much of herself to him as possible. They had been heady, exciting sensations.

She was surprised that any such yearning should emerge now, in the middle of the night, within walls that frightened her.

Was it because Mr. Brooke was both handsome and kind?

She shook her head. She should not

entertain such thoughts. The unexpected desire swirling in her loins must be because she had not been with a man in several years. As a dressing maid, she had few reasons to leave the Cameron residence and thus few opportunities to meet others. While she did relieve her lust from time to time at her own hand, it was not the same. Nature had imbued the human body with the need to mate.

She had lost her virtue in Barbados to a footman named Obadiah, but during a year when a fire destroyed half the sugar cane crop before harvest, he had been sold. After Obadiah, she had fallen in love with Solomon, a strapping young man who worked the fields, but he wanted his freedom above all else and had fled. Since arriving in England, she had not lain with a man. She missed the connection, the corporal excitement and relief, the joining of two bodies seeking the same end.

Daliyah rubbed her thighs together as Emma's cries grew in urgency. Their motions now sent her bed bumping into the wall. Emma cried out. A minute later, Mr. Brooke released a loud groan. The sounds ceased.

But the agitation inside Daliyah remained.

She slid her hand between her thighs and pressed upon the tension through her garments. It was an inconvenient time and place to attend her arousal, but it would not leave. She stroked herself lightly.

A few minutes later, however, she heard a door open. She heard footsteps—Mr. Brooke, she presumed—heading down the corridor.

Daliyah tried to return to sleep, tried to dash away the occasional vision of Mr. Brooke, of what he might look like sans clothing. He was not as majestic as Isaiah, whose daily labor in the fields had given him a strong and chiseled frame, but she liked the tender expression in Mr. Brooke's eyes. There was even a hint of sadness that she found kindred to her own.

Emma started to snore.

Daliyah returned her hand between her legs. After many, many long minutes, she found release and thought she finally might find repose. But sleep continued to elude her.

At least an hour must have passed when she heard footsteps again. Was Mr. Brooke returning to Emma? But these footsteps were lighter and continued down the corridor. It must be Jeremy or Mr. Phillips, who had the room at the end.

She went back to seeking her slumber when she heard shuffling and a thud. Perhaps Mr. Phillips had bumped against something in the dark. She recalled that she had not seen the light of a candle beneath her door when he had walked by. Why would he be walking about sans a candle in the middle of the night?

A part of her considered getting up and seeing if the man had hurt himself, but he would likely greet her with his usual surliness and possibly accuse her of spying upon him.

A shiver went through her at the sound of a wail.

It didn't ring in her ears but rather in her bones. She could not decide if she had indeed heard a sound or not. Listening carefully, she could only make out the sounds of Emma snoring and the weather outside. Perhaps she had heard a distant wolf or some poor prey of the wolf. Or perhaps she had simply imagined the cry.

But her pulse quickened and all the disquiet she had felt earlier returned twofold. She remained in bed, straining to hear more. After a few minutes, the footsteps returned to the corridor. Once again, she saw no light permeating the space beneath her door. Her heartbeat stalled.

The footsteps had stopped in front of her door.

Chapter Eight

*W*hy would Mr. Phillips wander the corridor in the dark? Daliyah wondered as she sat in her bed, her nerves on alert. If it was indeed Mr. Phillips. She could not be certain. Perhaps it was Jeremy or Mr. Brooke. She only knew that it could not be Emma, whose snoring she could still hear.

Though Daliyah could not see through the door, she felt as if whomever stood on the other side faced her, that it was not by chance that he happened to stop in front of her room.

"Hello?" she called out.

No response greeted her, but a minute later, the footsteps continued down the corridor.

A part of her was tempted to leap from her

bed and throw open the door to see who it was. Another part advised her to stay in the relative safety of her room.

Perhaps it was mere coincidence that the footsteps had stopped at her door. Perhaps Mr. Phillips had bumped his head and was disoriented.

The footsteps had sounded slow and deliberate, however.

Perhaps it was Jeremy up to some manner of mischief?

Several minutes passed, and Daliyah decided to settle back into bed. There was no cause for her to be so alarmed.

Before she lay down, however, the footsteps returned.

Thinking she might never fall asleep lest she put an end to the mysterious comings and goings, she hopped out of bed before fear could overtake her, lit her candle, and opened the door.

A startled Mr. Brooke, still in his attire from the day, turned around to face her and exclaimed, "Miss Daliyah!"

Realizing she had been holding her breath, she released it. "Mr. Brooke."

"Did I wake you?"

"No. I had not yet fallen asleep," she replied. "I heard a lot of walking, and a noise earlier made me wonder if Mr. Phillips had injured himself."

"Your pardon. I fear my pacing has been noisy."

"It was all you?" she asked, glancing in the direction of Mr. Phillips' room.

"I fear it so. I often have trouble sleeping, and I find that a walk quiets my state. But if my pacing disturbs you, I will desist."

"Pray, do not stop on my account, sir. I was merely curious as to who would be up at this hour of the night."

He smiled. "A person such as yourself?" When she looked down, he added, "It would seem we have in common the inability to sleep. Are your accommodations not comfortable enough?"

"They exceed expectation," she answered. "I normally share a room with one of the other housemaids. To have mine own were a luxury."

He appeared relieved. "If you require anything, do not hesitate to ask it of me."

"You are beyond kind, sir."

He seemed to appreciate her words, and their gazes briefly locked till a sound from upstairs made them both glance toward the stairwell. It had sounded like the closing of a door. Was the earl up as well?

She shivered, drawing Mr. Brooke's attention.

"You are cold," he said, his gaze taking in her shift. "I could procure for you another blanket."

"Pray, do not trouble yourself."

"Then you should take yourself to bed or you will catch cold. I fear this old castle can be damnably drafty."

"Then I bid you good night, Mr. Brooke."

He bowed. "Good night, Miss Daliyah."

She closed the door, then sighed. If only the Cameron servants were as gracious as Mr. Brooke. After climbing back into bed, she blew out the candle. This time she found herself becoming drowsy, but she did not slip into a deep sleep. At one point, as she floated in and out of consciousness, she thought she heard footsteps again. She supposed poor Mr. Brooke still could not sleep.

It had been silly of her to allow the footsteps to scare her as if some nefarious creature patrolled the corridor. She still found it strange that Mr. Brooke would pace the corridor sans any form of illumination, but he likely knew the quarters by heart. And though the first set of footsteps had sounded different in volume and cadence, she suspected she had merely heard wrong or Mr. Brooke had simply varied his walking.

Or perhaps Mr. Phillips had been up as well. As she drifted into sleep, she recalled seeing the door to his room had been left ajar.

*****

The following morning, Daliyah woke to hear Emma still snoring. The dimness outside the window suggested dawn had yet to break. Though Miss Cameron always slept late, Daliyah rose and dressed herself in the rare event that her mistress woke early and needed her.

After finishing her toilette, Daliyah stepped out into the corridor. Though still dark, it had none of the eeriness of the night. She glanced down the corridor and noticed that the door to Mr. Phillips' room was still ajar, even more than she remembered. Finding it odd, though she could not state why, she walked toward his room. Likely, he had simply forgotten to close it.

As she stood at the threshold, she sensed the room was empty. Perhaps because she heard neither snoring nor heavy breathing. She had no business standing here. Mr. Phillips would be livid to find her loitering about his room, but she was overcome with curiosity to see if her senses were right.

She considered whispering his name, but if he were asleep in his room, he would not be happy to be woken. Like Miss Cameron, he preferred to rise late. Half expecting a shoe to be thrown at her, Daliyah grabbed the door handle in case she needed to close the door quickly and peeked in.

She saw his bed. It was empty.

Releasing the handle, she realized her palm felt wet. She looked down at her hand and noticed a red smear. It looked like blood. She looked at the handle and saw nothing at first, but when she brushed her finger along the underside of the handle, she came away with more red. Holding the stain on her fingertip more closely to her gaze, she caught the metallic scent of blood.

Pushing the door wide open, she found Mr. Phillips nowhere in sight. She looked about for more bloodstains, evidence that Mr. Phillips had sustained an injury, but found none.

She went to the kitchen, where she wiped her hands and wondered if she should go looking for the driver, though Mr. Phillips would surely tell her to mind her own affairs.

"Are you always up this early?"

She gasped in surprise before whirling around to see Mr. Brooke at the threshold. Though he had faint circles beneath his eyes, he looked no less handsome.

"Forgive me," he said. "I startled you."

"A little," she acknowledged before glancing at his shirt sleeves. He had his coat draped over an arm.

Noticing her focus, he put on his coat. "Your pardon. I am not accustomed to having the fair sex about."

Daliyah felt her cheeks warm, though she had seen men—slaves only—shirtless before.

"No pardon is necessary," she replied.

"You told me yesterday you came from Barbados. How did you come to England?" he asked, stopping in front of the stove. "Would you care for coffee or tea?"

"Would you like me to boil a kettle of water for you, sir?" she asked as she reached for the kettle.

He, too, reached for the kettle, but she grasped it first, so his hand landed atop hers.

"I asked if you cared for coffee or tea," he said.

She stared at his hand, warm and strong, covering hers. She could not move her hand while it was trapped beneath his but found she did not want to. Unaccustomed to being asked what she wanted, she replied, "What do you desire, sir?"

He raised a brow. "Is my question so hard to answer?"

At a loss, she had no reply.

"Coffee? Or tea?" he asked again, before taking the kettle from her. "And I am quite capable of boiling water."

Did he mean to suggest he would make the tea or coffee himself? For her?

He checked the coal in the stove before starting a fire. "If you are undecided, Miss Daliyah, then I would suggest the tea. I have not been in town to purchase fresh grounds, and ours have become a bit bitter."

She watched him fill the kettle with water and set it on the stove.

"I fear we have few options for breakfast," he said, "but I suspect there are eggs in the hen house."

"Would you like me to procure them?"

"My dear, I would be an abominable host to pass my duties onto a guest."

"But..." She stopped, unsure what to say. Far more accustomed to receiving orders, she found herself in uncharted waters. What was the proper course of action?

Mr. Brooke eyed her keenly. "Have I distressed you?"

"No, no. I... It would be no imposition. I would rather be of service."

"If you insist, perhaps you could accompany me after we have had our tea. But first, you must answer at least one of my questions."

"Sir?"

"I first asked if you are always up this early, then asked how you came to England, before asking if you cared for coffee or tea. You haven't answered any of them."

She flushed. With Mr. Brooke in it, the kitchen felt small.

"I like the quiet of the morning," she answered. "And I believe you decided on tea."

Mr. Brooke smiled. "I did, but I can just as easily make coffee if you prefer."

"Do you prefer coffee?"

"I do, but I do not mind it bitter."

"Then I will make you coffee, sir."

"Are you always this difficult?"

She balked in surprise. How was she being difficult?

Sensing her question, he said, "You would insist on being the host, though you are the guest here."

"But I'm…"

Did he truly not understand? As an indentured servant, she had but one purpose: to serve all those above her.

"Presumptuous?" he filled in.

Her mouth dropped at his impertinence. For being courteous and obsequious, she was being called presumptuous?

"Your pardon," he said. "That was uncalled for. But I hope you will hence relinquish your compulsion to reverse our roles."

"If that is what you wish, sir," she said carefully, uncertain if what she said was best.

"It is. Now, how did you come to England?"

"I was indentured to a ship captain for passage to England. My covenant was sold to Mr. Cameron a year after I arrived."

"How long is your indenture?"

"Five years, but I have completed nearly four."

"Only a year remains before you can rejoice, then."

She nodded.

"Do you plan to return to Barbados or does England compare favorably enough for you to stay?"

She hesitated, for the truth was that she missed Barbados. She had neither family nor friends in England, and she found no joy in serving the Cameron family. Her solace was that in England, she did not have to witness the horrors of plantation life on a daily basis or have her heart broken to hear of slaves punished and killed for daring to taste of freedom.

"The two are quite different," she offered, not wanting to prevaricate but not wishing to offend Mr. Brooke.

"Tell me more of Barbados. I've never been anywhere beyond England."

She hesitated, unsure what to make of the conversation she was having. While she found it exciting to converse with someone who seemed to take an interest in her, she felt herself in unfamiliar territory.

But the kettle whistled just then. She went to get it, but he stopped her.

"Allow me," he said. "If you would kindly take a seat at the table, it would please me to serve you tea."

Given that directive, she had no choice but to do as he bid if she did not wish to appear defiant. As she sat down, she recalled that she had not seen Mr. Phillips about. She asked if Mr. Brooke had seen the man.

Mr. Brooke had his back turned to her, but it seemed he stiffened for a moment before taking the kettle off the stove.

"He went to the posting inn to procure a fresh set of horses," Mr. Brooke replied as he prepared a teapot.

Her eyes widened. "Alone? What of the wolves?"

"They are not known to appear in the

morning. They begin hunting only when it is nearer to night."

"Mr. Phillips left quite early," Daliyah reflected aloud.

"It seemed your mistress is in some hurry to arrive in London."

It made sense, then, that Mr. Phillips had risen and departed early.

"Did you notice if he was injured?" she asked.

"I had not. Why do you ask?"

She watched as Mr. Brooke picked up the pot of tea to place upon a tray, saying, "I found droplets of blood upon his—"

But she was interrupted by the teapot crashing to the floor.

Chapter Nine

Addison cursed as hot water splashed up to his breeches. Miss Daliyah rushed over to assist in picking up the broken pieces.

"Pray, leave it be. It is my carelessness to attend," he said, bending down after her. His hand grazed hers as they reached for the same shard, and he recalled how soft her hand had felt beneath his when they had both reached for the kettle. He had deliberately kept his hand upon hers longer than appropriate.

Meeting his gaze, she said, "It would please me to be of assistance, sir."

He did not wave her off and allowed her to help in picking up the pieces of the teapot and placing them onto the tray. She spotted a broom and retrieved it to sweep up the smaller pieces while he disposed of the broken teapot and found a new one.

How had he missed the blood?

Last night, after Miss Daliyah had startled him in the corridor, he had retreated back to his own room and waited for what he hoped was sufficient time for her to fall asleep. As he could not wait till morning to dispose of the body, he made another attempt down the corridor, stopping before Miss Daliyah's door to see if she would come out once more. When she did not, he had proceeded to Mr. Phillips' room.

Montague had told him that Mr. Phillips had put up a stronger fight than expected and even managed to sink his teeth into Montague's hand, piercing his skin, before Montague managed to break the man's neck.

In the dark, Addison had wrapped the body of Mr. Phillips, along with the man's shoes and coat, in a blanket and carried it outside. In the wind and rain, he had dug a grave. After returning to the castle and changing into dry clothes, he had returned to Mr. Phillips' room, this time with a candle, to inspect if any droplets of blood might have fallen on the bedclothes or the floor. Montague did not often leave evidence, but apparently Addison had not been thorough enough in his inspection.

"You say you found blood?" he asked.

"Only a little. Upon the door handle."

"'Tis easy enough for anyone to cut their hand."

"Yes. Allow me to make the tea," Miss Daliyah offered, "whilst you attend to your garments."

He nodded, glad for the opportunity to leave her question unanswered. Instead of heading straightway to his own quarters, however, he went to the room of Mr. Phillips. With his handkerchief, he wiped down the door handle and looked about for more blood. He then went in and reviewed the room. Satisfied that nothing else appeared amiss, he returned to his own quarters to change.

The other two Cameron servants were still asleep, and he was glad to have the sole company of Miss Daliyah. She gave him a small smile when he entered the kitchen. He saw that she had on the table a cup of tea and a cup of coffee.

"Alas, I am an incompetent host," he remarked as they sat at the table.

"You have been beyond kind and beyond reproach," she objected.

Sitting across from her, he marveled once more at both the largeness and the brightness of her eyes.

"I believe you were to tell me of Barbados," he said.

"What do you wish to know?"

"Anything."

"Well, unlike England, it is often warm and humid. The size and strength of the sun is much more formidable in Barbados."

"Is it difficult to bear?"

"At times, especially in the fields."

"The fields?"

"I lived upon a sugarcane plantation."

"Were you a dressing maid there?"

"A house maid, like my mother before me."

"Is she here in England with you?"

"She died in childbirth. I was raised by my grandmother, and she passed away a year before I left for England."

"Have you any family? A husband, perhaps?"

She shook her head before looking down.

"Why did you wish to come to England?" he asked.

"I came to see my father. He took ill in Barbados, and his physician advised him to return to England, but when I arrived, I learned that he had passed away."

"I am sorry for your loss. You are all alone here in England, then?"

Looking at him, she seemed surprised by his sympathy. "You ask a great many questions, Mr. Brooke."

"Do you find me prying? I can cease."

"I take no offense. No one has simply ever asked so many of me before."

He wanted to offer her a turn at asking, but the last thing he wanted was to face questions he might not wish to answer.

"You must tell me how a dressing maid came to have such a sure hand with horses," he said.

"Luck, I should think."

He shook his head. "A natural talent with animals, rather."

"I would I had a way with the wolves we encountered in the forest," she said with a shiver.

He pressed his lips into a grim line before

saying, "Those wolves are the devil's creation. I am sorry you came under their attack."

"We are grateful to have sighted Castle Blackbourne when we did."

Addison shifted in discomfort. Their lot with the wolves would not have been better, but it would not have been worse.

"Would you care for more coffee, sir?" she asked.

He wanted to have another cup and continue conversing at the table, but he replied that there were eggs to be gotten and the animals to be fed.

"If you think your mistress will not need you," he added, "I would be much obliged for the company."

The words were out of his mouth before he could contemplate the wisdom of his actions, but even if he had time or opportunity to reconsider, he might still choose to do the same. He enjoyed her presence and found her comely, though forming any attachment, no matter how minimal or short in length, would only serve to make her demise more painful.

"How is it you manage an entire castle by yourself?" she asked while she dropped feed for the chickens and he milked the cow.

"A great many of the rooms are unused and permitted to gather dust," he answered, "and his lordship requires little attention aside from his shave and dress."

"Does he rise later in the mornings?"

He almost said that Montague preferred the dark of night but managed to reply with a simple, "Aye. How did you come by the name 'Daliyah'? I've never heard its like before."

"My grandmother told me it is a name from her village and that a great *sangoma* bore the name."

"What is a *sangoma*?"

"One who heals. If you are amenable, I should like to look upon the injured horse."

"I think she would be happy to receive a visit from you."

Miss Daliyah seemed to blush, making her even more lovely in Addison's eyes. When they had collected a few eggs and he finished with milking the cow, he showed her to the stables.

"The other horses are still here," she noticed. "I wonder that Mr. Phillips did not take them if he meant to exchange the horses for a new team?"

Damnation. Addison searched for a plausible

reasoning.

"I told him to leave them," he said. "With one of them injured, it does no good to have only three returned. They are accustomed to pulling together."

She appeared to accept his explanation and went to stroke the horses. As he collected the oats to feed them, he observed how the animals, skittish in their hunger, seemed to calm in her presence. He appreciated that she did not complain about the smell of mud mixed with horse manure and discerned an impressive level of stoicism within her. Though he barely knew her, he sensed she had many a good quality.

It was a shame she would not be much longer upon this earth.

Chapter Ten

Being noon, the sun was high in the sky. Despite the thickness of the curtains, the light managed to sneak around them. Montague despaired that the rain clouds had not lingered. With every passing year, he disliked the sunlight more and more. It was a sign of his demise.

But perhaps Miss Cameron was to be his salvation. After his years of wallowing in blood and thirst, Fate had finally taken pity upon his soul and seen fit to send him some fortune.

A knock at the door prompted him to stir. Knowing it to be Addison, he replied, "Enter."

Addison brought in a tray of tea and set it upon a table. This, despite the fact that

Montague had lost any interest in all fluids save that of blood, Addison did without fail every morning—or afternoon, as it were—a habit from the days before the curse, or perhaps a gesture of hope to the return of that normalcy.

"How do you fare?" Addison asked.

They had not spoken during the night. After feeding, Montague had stopped in Addison's room simply to let his brother know that he was done. Montague rarely spoke after feeding, an act that left him feeling more beast than human. Words, therefore, would have been out of place.

"You look far better," Addison noted.

"I feel far better," Montague said as he went to sit in a chair for his morning shave. Noting the shadow beneath Addison's eyes, he asked, "Was it difficult disposing of the body?"

Addison prepared the razor and shaving cream, answering, "Because of the rains, I thought it wise to dig a deeper grave. And I had a brief delay when I came across Miss Daliyah."

"Miss Daliyah?"

"She heard me walking in the corridor and came out of her room."

Montague recalled that he had suspected the

maid to be awake. Though she could not see through the door, she had addressed him. Or perhaps she merely talked in her sleep. But as he stood in front of the room, contemplating whether or not to take her that night, he had felt her wakefulness and even scented her fear, an aroma that intoxicated and fueled his hunger for both flesh and blood.

He remembered the spike of fear in Mr. Phillips when his fangs had sunk into his neck. Confused at first, the driver knew then that what was being perpetrated upon him was no jest or misunderstanding, but malice.

The man had fought harder than Montague had expected. When his hand had slipped from the servant's mouth, rather than scream for help, he had chosen to bite down upon Montague.

"You hurt yourself," Addison noticed of the bandages Montague had wrapped about his hand.

"A minor flesh wound," Montague replied.

The bite, however, had changed his plans. He knew not what poison exuded from his fangs, but when he sank them into his prey, it seemed he infused them with his own lust. They became willing participants to their own rape.

Montague had fully intended to bugger Mr. Phillips as he fed upon him. But he did not want to risk more noise and fighting, so he had drilled his fist into Mr. Phillips, knocking the man out before draining him of his life.

Having satisfied one hunger but not the other, he had stopped in front of Miss Daliyah's room as he considered satiating his other craving. But if he were to take her, he would have to drain her too. And the disappearance of two servants would raise too much suspicion.

"What pretense shall we provide for the disappearance of Miss Daliyah?" he wondered aloud. "Perhaps she could be sent into town? I could wait for her in the forest."

In the midst of drawing the razor down Montague's cheek, Addison paused. "It has been but half a day since you fed."

"And weeks in which I starved. Mr. Phillips was but half a feast, and barely that. But it is the other appetite I need attended."

Even if he had fucked Mr. Phillips, Montague much preferred ravishing the fair sex.

"In truth, I never feel fully satiated," he

sighed. "I could feed and ravish an army yet still some modicum of thirst remains."

"What of the other maid?"

"The one you fucked?"

"Her cunnie were sweet." Addison resumed shaving. "But perhaps all this need not come to pass if we can undo the curse."

"I stayed up most of the night reading by candlelight and came across nothing."

"If only we could find a witch. Perhaps we should renew our search now that we have the beauty."

In addition to his own time and that of Addison's, Montague had spent thousands of pounds paying others to search for the witch who had cursed him. Her parting words to him, which he had deemed nonsense at the time, were somehow seared into his memory. He had repeated them and torn them apart in search of clues so often that Addison, too, knew them by heart.

"Yes," agreed Montague. "The one who cursed me could be oceans away, but perhaps any witch might be of use."

"In the meantime, perhaps the blood of Mr. Phillips could keep you satisfied enough for a spell."

"Have I not always attempted to rein in my appetites for as long as possible?" Montague returned. "In the end, the hunger always wins."

"I know it," Addison said quietly.

"To have the temptation so near to me only makes it more difficult to resist."

"There is the footman, if you feel you must feed again."

"You intend to fuck the maid again? I suppose I could leave her to the very end."

As the blade scratched across his skin, Montague waited for Addison to express his appreciation, but he did not. Done with the shave, he asked instead, "Then you will avail yourself of the footman next if your urges prove too strong?"

Montague waited for Addison to wipe away all the shaving cream before standing up and replying, "I would rather not bugger a footman when there is cunnie to be had."

Looking down, Addison seemed in thought as he cleaned the blade.

"I think you would do the same were you in my place," Montague added as he took off his nightshirt and prepared to dress.

"I would I could take your place," Addison mourned.

It was not the first time Addison had voiced the sentiment. He knew that Addison would endure any pain rather than see Montague suffer it.

Once, when Addison was seven and Montague twelve, the Duke and Duchess of Winingham had stayed at Castle Blackbourne as guests of the earl. Montague's father had been courting the friendship of Winingham for many years, and it was an honor for the earl to host the duke. The duchess had brought with her a small Maltese, whose care she left to Montague when the adults went out for the foxhunt. Montague and Addison were playing cricket when Montague accidentally hit the ball into the dog, striking the animal between the eyes. It had died instantly. The duchess was devastated.

Addison had confessed to killing the dog, for which he was soundly beaten.

"If you prefer me to make the footman my next victim, then I will attempt to honor your wishes," Montague said.

Addison nodded and his mood seemed to

lighten. He assisted Montague into his attire before leaving to attend his other chores.

Dressed and groomed, Montague, to appear a good host, went to inquire after Miss Cameron. She was taking a late breakfast in her chambers and seemed in good spirits to receive him.

"I pray your night here was sufficiently comfortable," Montague said after taking a chair opposite her. "If there is anything you require, do not hesitate to ask it of me or Mr. Brooke."

She gave him a bright smile. "You are a most gracious host, your lordship. And I wish to apologize once more for the atrocious behavior of my maid. In truth, I know not why my father chose to purchase her service. I think she did not please her previous employer, and my father took her off their hands as a favor. My father once contemplated moving to the West Indies. Heavens! Can you imagine?"

Thinking how brightly the sun must burn in that part of the world, Montague acknowledged he could not.

"My father heard that some of the slaves there conspire to overthrow their owners, and there are so many of them there, I should fear for my life every day. And even were there not so many, I should still prefer England. I find that London does have more of their kind, including ones who walk about as free as an Englishman. Sometimes I wonder if our society is regressing."

While Miss Cameron prattled on topics Montague found rather inane, and as he found her insights and wits middling at best, he pondered how she might break the curse for him. He had fed on women of beauty before, but they had done nothing for him. What could he do differently with Miss Cameron? Marry her? Perform some witches' ritual? By God, he would do anything to rid himself of this curse.

"You are in some hurry, then?" he asked when Miss Cameron mentioned that they were already days behind in their travels.

She reconsidered. "I suppose if my aunt has waited this long, a few more days would make little difference."

"If your driver is unable to secure a proper team of horses, know that you are more than welcome to stay at Castle Blackbourne for as long as you need."

"Ah! You are true kindness, my lord!"

Having endured enough of her company, he rose, bowed, and reiterated that he was at her service. He opened the door but turned around when she called out to him.

"And should you need the service of any of my servants, I am certain they would only be too happy to assist your Mr. Brooke," she said.

He thanked her and, turning to leave, stepped right into Miss Daliyah, who carried a tray of milk, tea, jam, and biscuits. The milk splashed onto her face and hair. She fumbled the tray, attempted to catch the jam, only to have it spill over her hand before it and the rest of the contents fell to the floor.

Rushing over, Miss Cameron cried out, "Daliyah! How careless of you!" She looked Montague over. "Did she spill anything upon you?"

"No," he answered. "I believe she bore the brunt of it, but it was my fault. I did not look where I was headed."

"Not at all," Miss Cameron objected as her maid wiped the milk from her face and bent down to retrieve the fallen items. "It was Daliyah who failed to observe where she was going." Miss Cameron frowned at the maid. "Now look at the mess you've made!"

"I will have Mr. Brooke tend to it," Montague said, "so that your maid can cleanse herself."

"How indebted we are to you and Mr. Brooke."

Having put everything back on the tray, Miss Daliyah said to her mistress, "Forgive me. I will bring a new tray."

Miss Cameron pursed her lips. "Have Emma bring it. I will not tolerate another spill from you."

Miss Daliyah turned to leave. Milk dripped from her bonnet into her eyes, and she took a misstep. Montague, following her, reached out to steady her.

Warmth seared through his hand, and he had to forcibly loosen his grip upon her arm. He took the tray from her so that she could more fully wipe the milk from herself.

"Come, child, I will assist you," he said.

"Truly, Daliyah!" Miss Cameron scolded. "What trouble you have caused, and we have been here hardly a day!"

"I assure you it is no trouble," Montague told her.

The memory of how the maid felt in his hand lingered. His fangs threatened to lengthen, and he quickly turned to take his leave of Miss Cameron.

Following him, the maid said, "I beg your pardon, my lord, for the inconveniences I have imposed. If you will, I can take the tray now."

She looked a sorry state with drops of milk still in her hair and the stain of tea and jam over the front of her dress. He wondered how old she was. He suspected her to be rather young, given her supple and unblemished complexion. With bright eyes, thick lashes, and a fine symmetry of features, though her lips were plumper than what was considered enviable, she was surprisingly comely. She seemed possessed of a fine figure as well, sufficiently full in the bosom but slender in the arms.

Desire flamed in his loins.

Feeling his fangs once more, he quickly handed her the tray and instructed, "Find Mr. Brooke. Then you may tend to yourself."

"Yes, my lord."

She could not depart fast enough for him. Though his appetite should have significantly abated after he had fed upon Mr. Phillips, the scent of the maid had renewed his hunger—both of them.

The stupid girl. If she had not dropped her tray, he would not have had cause to stand so close to her or touch her.

Covering his mouth, he retreated to his own chambers, where he took several deep breaths in an attempt to calm his ardor.

Though he had told Addison that he would refrain from preying upon one of the maids, he doubted he could last the night. And as Miss Cameron seemed displeased with the maid, it made sense for him to choose her next.

Chapter Eleven

"Your pardon, Miss Daliyah!" Mr. Brooke said.

Daliyah kept her gaze averted, as she had come upon Mr. Brooke sans coat *and* shirt. Trying not to dwell on the chiseled features of his chest and abdomen, she said, "I shall return at a later time."

"Stay," he said, setting down the axe he had been using to chop wood to pick up his shirt and coat. "I had not thought anyone would come outside."

"I'm sorry to inconvenience you," she said as she continued to stare at the tub she carried, containing the dress she had washed of tea and jam as well as a few articles of Miss Cameron's.

"It would not have been an inconvenience had I the forethought to keep my shirt and coat. I am still unaccustomed to having guests. Now that I am proper, may I assist you?"

Looking up, she replied, "I only came to hang these garments out to dry while there is a little sunlight left in the day."

"You may use the clothesline there," he indicated.

After she had pinned her dress, she returned to where Mr. Brooke had resumed chopping the wood.

"I wonder that Mr. Phillips has not yet returned?" she asked. She had hoped that the driver would have returned with the necessary team of horses well before noon and that they might have been on their way a few hours later. She still felt unsettled here at Castle Blackbourne.

"Perhaps he was unable to secure the horses from the nearest posting inn and had to try another," Mr. Brooke replied before bringing the axe down upon a log. "Or perhaps he met a friend."

He did not sound concerned, which comforted her a little. Daliyah would not have put it past Mr. Phillips to partake of a few mugs of ale if he could, but he would know better than to be too long about it.

"Do the wolves not come out when it is near night?" she asked.

With the back of his sleeve, he wiped the perspiration from his brow "They do, but I suspect Mr. Phillips will be returned before then."

"I hope so. How far is the second nearest posting inn?"

Mr. Brooke appeared slightly uncomfortable and kept his eyes upon the log he had split before replying, "Within a reasonable distance."

"You don't think it too far?"

"Er, no."

"I did not happen to see another posting inn on the main road in town," she recalled aloud.

"It were...it is an unremarkable structure, rather small."

Apparently intent on chopping wood, he picked up another log.

"Do you think he might be lost?" she inquired.

Mr. Brooke sighed, she could not tell from exertion or exasperation.

"Your Mr. Phillips seems an intelligent and resourceful man," Mr. Brooke said as he collected the wood, "and quite capable of handling himself."

She nodded. Perhaps she fretted needlessly.

But another hour passed, and still Mr. Phillips had not returned. Then two hours passed.

To keep from fretting excessively, she kept herself busy. She offered to feed and tend the horses. She repaired the lace that had come off of one of Miss Cameron's gloves. She would have liked to converse again with Mr. Brooke as they had in the early hours of the morning, but Emma occupied his attentions.

When a third hour passed with no sign of Mr. Phillips, Daliyah decided she should broach the matter with Miss Cameron, who no longer seemed to be in a hurry to reach London.

"What have you learned from Mr. Brooke about his master?" Miss Cameron asked Emma while the maids assisted her with her evening dress. "I had a lovely stroll about the gardens with his lordship this afternoon, and I think he and I suit each other quite well. But I must know more about him. The gardens were in a frightful state of neglect, and I can only think that finances prevent him from retaining the services of a gardener."

"That he is an only child and sole heir of the previous Earl of Blackbourne," Emma replied as she applied herself to Miss Cameron's coiffure.

"I will have the rubies," Miss Cameron said to Daliyah after being shown her jewelry collection. "I think the hue of rubies to complement my coloring."

Daliyah kept the ruby earrings and necklace before putting away the rest.

"And does the earl have assets beyond Castle Blackbourne?" Miss Cameron asked.

"He has a house in London but rarely stays there, according to Mr. Brooke."

"Where in Town? Mayfair?"

"Grosvenor Square."

At that, Miss Cameron smiled. "What of the dowager? Where is she?"

"The late countess passed when he was young."

"Did Mr. Brooke indicate what his lordship's income might be?"

Emma shook her head.

"And why does he keep only the one

servant?"

"Mr. Brooke said that his lordship prefers solitude. He finds the comings and goings of servants to be quite distracting."

"His lordship had said as much, but I find it hard to think of him as a recluse as he seems quite amiable."

Though Daliyah found Lord Blackbourne sufficiently courteous, she would not have described him as *amiable.* There was an aloofness, a coldness, to his mien. His touch, after she had spilled the tray earlier in the day, seemed to have seeped through her sleeve, sending a chill through her. And it surprised her none at all that he preferred less company to more.

She had also noticed that his hand had been bandaged. It reminded her of the blood she had found on Mr. Phillips' door, but that was surely a coincidence. Lord Blackbourne would have no cause to be in the servants' quarters.

"Mr. Phillips has yet to return," Daliyah remarked, "and he left quite early in the morning."

She had given up hope that they would depart today, and she dreaded spending another night at Castle Blackbourne, but her chief worry was that something had happened to Mr. Phillips.

"That is odd," Miss Cameron said. "But what is there to be done? Now which of these fragrances should I apply? Do you think Lord Blackbourne would favor the one with amber notes or the orange blossom?"

"They are both of them quite fine," Emma replied.

"Oh, and as Daliyah has been quite the clumsy dolt today, I think it best if you served his lordship and me at dinner."

Daliyah was glad to be relieved of any duty that would put her in the way of Lord Blackbourne. She had caught him looking at her from the mezzanine near the stairs. His gaze had chilled her to the bones. It was rather extraordinary that such a master would have such a warm and friendly manservant in Mr. Brooke.

In the kitchen, Mr. Brooke was already preparing the dinner.

"I hope your mistress will not mind having stew and potatoes for a second night," he said.

"I cannot speak for her, but she is presently

in good spirits," Daliyah replied.

"That is good to hear," he said with genuine pleasure.

Jeremy sat at the kitchen table, slicing an apple for himself. "Have you any more blankets to spare? The temperature in this castle plummets at night, and I swear a blast of cold air blew through my room last night."

"I can bring you additional bedclothing. Remind me if I forget."

"I wonder that your master can stand living in this place if he has a townhouse in London."

"Are you well, Miss Daliyah?"

Busy calculating how much time might remain before the wolves appeared, she was not aware of Mr. Brooke's study of her.

"I worry of Mr. Phillips," she confessed. "What if he has injured himself in the woods? What if he fell from his horse?"

"Do the wolves come out every night?" Jeremy asked.

"They do," answered Mr. Brooke. He turned to Daliyah. "You are quite distressed about him?"

She nodded.

"Then I will have a look about the woods if

one of you can attend to the dinner."

"I've no notion how to cook," Jeremy said.

"I can," Daliyah said, giving Mr. Brooke a look of gratitude.

He received it with a smile.

After he had left, Emma walked into the kitchen, asking, "Where is Mr. Brooke?"

"He is headed out in search of Mr. Phillips," Jeremy answered.

She took a seat near Jeremy. "He has been gone for some time."

"Mr. Phillips likely drank himself into a stupor and has not yet woken from it." That seemed to give him an idea, for he asked, "I wonder what they have in the way of drink about here?"

Getting up, he looked around the kitchen. Finding nothing, he said to Daliyah, "Have a look about the wine cellar and bring something up for us."

If she could speak her mind without repercussions, she would have asked Jeremy why he did not go himself. She suspected he did not wish for himself to be caught pilfering from the cellar.

"What are you waiting for?" Emma snapped.

"I know not where the cellar may be," Daliyah said.

Jeremy pointed to a thick wooden door just outside the kitchen. "Likely through that door."

"And we should ask Mr. Brooke—"

Jeremy narrowed his eyes. "Are you stupid? Mr. Brooke is far too proper a servant to allow us to partake of his master's cellar."

"Then we should not."

"If he discovers you, simply tell him you needed wine for the stew."

"But still we should ask first—"

Jeremy folded his arms in front of him. "You want to cross us, do you?"

Emma added, "I wonder what Mr. Cameron would do if he were to discover what a poor maid you have been to his daughter?"

He replied to Emma, "Sell her, he would. Perhaps to the likes of Mr. Flynn. He keeps a great many maids and seems partial to the younger ones."

Daliyah felt her cheeks burn. Without word, she turned around and headed to the door Jeremy had pointed to earlier. She pulled upon the iron latch, but the door was too heavy. Jeremy had to assist her.

When even he could not open it, she suggested they give up. But Jeremy went back to the kitchen and retrieved an iron poker.

"You pry open the door with this while I pull upon the latch," he instructed.

After several attempts, they succeeded. With the door opened, the air from behind it seemed to escape with a moan. She saw nothing but stairs that descended into darkness.

"Are you certain the cellar be down there?" she asked Jeremy, who had followed her and peered over her shoulder.

"Why not?" he returned. He called to Emma. "Fetch a candelabra."

"Fetch it yourself," Emma retorted.

With a huff, Jeremy went into the kitchen to retrieve the candelabra, which he then handed to Daliyah. "Go on, then."

But Daliyah hesitated. The air felt of malice and desperation to her.

"Go on!" Jeremy scolded.

Bracing her nerves, she descended the stairs, slowly. Unlike the kitchen, the stone walls of the stairwell likely belonged to the original structure of the castle.

She wondered what she was afraid of. Mice?

Back in Barbados, she had come across many in the sugarcane fields. The dark itself? But that was nonsense.

Nevertheless, her breath quivered when she exhaled. The stairwell curved so that she could no longer see the top of the stairs where Jeremy stood and seemed to extend quite a ways below.

When she finally reached the bottom, she saw a closed door to her left. Could that be the wine cellar?

Closing her eyes, Daliyah heard the voice of her grandmother. *Feel the air. Listen to it. What does it say?*

Daliyah believed it said not to open the door. Looking farther down the corridor, Daliyah saw another door on the right side. Of the same construction as the first, it comprised thick wooden boards reinforced with iron. Both had a small window with bars near the top. She had never seen their like before. A third door appeared open.

Thinking that could be the cellar, she sauntered over.

Peering in, she felt the blood drain from her.

There were no racks of wine, nor kegs of ale. Instead, all she saw were skeletons. Human skeletons. More than half a dozen, a few piled atop another, and a few others strewn upon the ground.

Stifling a cry, she quickly turned around and hurried back up the stairs.

But when she reached the top, she found the door closed. She pushed upon it. It did not budge. Why would Jeremy have closed the door on her? She pushed harder but to no avail. She pounded on the door and called to Jeremy. He did not answer.

The air seemed to grow colder, more ominous. It seemed as if the skeletons below called to her, or perhaps they warned her. But she discerned nothing certain save her desperation to be free. She leaned her shoulder against the wall and pushed with all her might.

"Jeremy!" she tried again.

But the door remained closed.

She was trapped.

Chapter Twelve

Having forgotten to tell Miss Daliyah that, lest she still had biscuits and jam, there would be naught to serve for dessert, Addison decided to return to the kitchen before heading out in his feigned search for Mr. Phillips. As he proceeded down the corridor, he thought he heard a door close and came upon Jeremy.

"I thought you had gone to find Mr. Phillips," the footman said.

"I am about to," Addison replied, "but I wish to have a word with Miss Daliyah before I go."

"We are all rather worried about Mr. Phillips, as it seems he has been gone for nearly the entire day. Perhaps I can convey your word to Miss Daliyah so that you need not tarry."

Jeremy sounded oddly eager to be of service, a quality Addison had not suspected the young man to possess.

"Very well. I merely wish to inform her that there is nothing in the way of dessert to be served, but that I will go into town the morrow and purchase a pie or cake for dinner."

"Is that necessary? We might be on our way before dinner."

Addison hesitated before replying, "Quite right."

He turned to leave but stopped when he thought he heard thudding. Turning back around, he asked Jeremy, "What is that?"

"Hm? To what do you refer, Mr. Brooke?"

Addison strained to hear. The thudding continued. "That sound."

Jeremy returned a quizzical look.

How did he not hear? Addison wondered as he walked in the direction of the sound.

"Has some animal got into the castle, perhaps?" Jeremy inquired.

The sound grew louder as Addison neared the door that led down to the dungeon. What the devil...?

Standing before the door, there was no denying the pounding from behind it and the muffled cries of help. Grabbing onto the latch, he quickly heaved the door open. Miss Daliyah tumbled into his arms.

How did she end up there? *Why* was she there?

But he set aside the questions in favor of holding Miss Daliyah, who shivered against him. Despite the questionable propriety, she held onto his arms, not unlike a scared child seeking comfort and safety from an adult. Her eyes were closed, as if she were afraid of what she might see.

Addison wondered with dread if she had she seen the contents of the dungeon.

"Miss Daliyah, are you unwell?" he asked. Despite his concerns, he could not help but enjoy the feel of her in his arms. He wanted to hold her closer and wrap her in a comforting embrace.

"What were you doing down there, Daliyah?" Jeremy asked. "I thought you were in the kitchen?"

Realizing where she was, Miss Daliyah pulled away. She looked at Jeremy. Addison caught him giving her a stern look.

"I thought the stew might benefit from some wine," she said, her voice slightly trembling.

"That door leads not to the cellar," he informed her, picking up the candle she had dropped and handing it back to her. "Are you certain you are well? Perhaps I should stay and make the dinner?"

"No! You must go in search of Mr. Phillips. I will be fine."

He searched her countenance and saw clearly that she was still shaken.

"No one has gone down there in decades," he lied, for the dungeon was where Montague once consumed his victims. "It is a part of the castle that ceased to be of use long ago."

"There w-were remains…"

"It was once a dungeon."

"Indeed?" Jeremy asked with interest.

Emma, who had wandered over to attend the commotion, gasped. She looked at Miss Daliyah. "Did you see…skeletons?"

Miss Daliyah nodded.

"I am terribly sorry that you had to endure a most wretched history of the castle. It was built two hundred years ago, you see. I remember, as a child, wandering down there by accident and having nightmares for several sennights thereafter. But why did you close the door behind you?"

"I didn't," Miss Daliyah replied. "It—it must have closed of its own accord."

In the dozens of trips Addison had made down to the dungeon, the door had never once closed upon him. He looked at Jeremy with suspicion.

"Allow me to procure the wine you seek," he said to Miss Daliyah, "and I will finish making the dinner."

"Pray, do not. While it was an unpleasant sight, the unknown state of Mr. Phillips distresses me more."

At that, Addison felt he had little choice but to leave her to finish the cooking. He gave Jeremy one more look to make it known to the footman that he was watching him. Addison doubted the footman would attempt the jest again, now that Miss Daliyah was the wiser.

"I hope not to be long," he told her after handing her the wine. He silently scolded himself for forgetting to lock the door to the dungeon.

"Thank you," she replied.

She truly had the brightest eyes he had ever seen, he decided, as their gazes briefly met. He wanted to press her on the true reason she had ended up in the stairwell to the dungeon. He did not think cooking to be the only motive. Why did she not lay any of the blame upon Jeremy? Was she also guilty or was it not in her nature to tattle on a fellow servant?

Addison imagined Jeremy threatening her if she told the truth, a likelihood that would not have surprised Addison given the treatment he had witnessed. The thought made him angry.

He saddled his horse and took his musket with him in his charade. He rode till he was far enough from view but within easy riding distance should the wolves be out early this evening.

Sensing his master had no destination in mind, his horse began wandering and sniffed at the grass.

Looking to the sky, he saw that the clouds had returned. The earlier sunlight had been a rare show of brightness. Like Miss Daliyah. There was no artifice to her courtesy but warmth and generosity in her spirit. He felt confident of this despite having known her less than four and twenty hours. The more he looked upon her, the lovelier she became. Even if she had not the beauty of Miss Cameron, he was surprised he preferred Miss Daliyah.

Montague had said he would refrain from taking any of the maids. If the time came when he could no longer hold back his appetites, Addison found he hoped his brother would choose Miss Emma. He himself had thought to bed her again. She had hinted at it twice today. But it would hardly be fair for him to indulge his carnal desires when Montague could not.

After waiting in the forest for what he deemed sufficient enough time to constitute a thorough search for Mr. Phillips, Addison returned to the castle. As he turned his horse around, a wolf howled in the near distance.

Addison remembered his worst encounter with the beasts. He had gone into town and procured a victim for Montague, who had been too weak to hunt for one himself. Addison had pleaded for Montague to stop his feeding, and Montague had tried, but when his brother appeared to be on Death's doorstep, Addison could take it no longer. After riding into town, he had found an elderly drunkard and convinced the man that there was work to be had at the castle. Returning late, they had come upon three of the wolves. After shooting one of the beasts, Addison could not load his musket fast enough. The other two had descended upon them, ready to tear them to pieces.

Montague had appeared then. In addition to his horrid appetites, the curse had given him uncommon strength. He had managed to toss one against a tree, giving Addison time to finish loading his musket with powder and shot. He had killed the third wolf, but not before it had mangled the drunkard. In his hunger, Montague had seemed not to care. He had descended upon the poor man, whose own howls pierced the night as loudly as those of the wolves.

Arriving back at the castle, he informed the others that he was, regretfully, unable to find Mr. Phillips in the woods and would go into town the following morning in search of the driver.

"I should not have waited so long to go in search of him," he lamented, though his true regret was bringing disappointment to Miss

Daliyah's eyes.

"You could not have known he would not return," she said.

She seemed to have recovered from her foray into the dungeon, though Addison still wished it had been Jeremy who had been trapped instead.

Miss Cameron and Montague had retired to the drawing room after dinner. Addison found Montague at the harpsichord while Miss Cameron sang.

"Your voice is a delight," Montague praised when she had finished.

Pleased, she returned the compliment. "And your playing quite commendable, my lord."

"You are too kind. In truth, it has been many years since I have touched the instrument, and I was quite the poor pupil. I think my music instructor dreaded the days he had lessons with me."

Miss Cameron giggled. "I can imagine you as a mischievous sort of young lad."

Spotting Addison, Montague said, "You have news of Mr. Phillips?"

Addison stepped forward. "I know not if it be good or bad that I could not find him. He must still be in town, and I will venture there as soon as I can in the morning."

"Then I fear we shall have to trespass upon your hospitality another night," Miss Cameron said to Montague.

"I more than welcome the opportunity to be of service," he replied.

Back in the servants' quarters, Addison had a late supper while he watched as Daliyah cleaned the kitchen. He ate quickly, for he wanted to assist her and escape the presence of Emma, who continued to pepper him with questions about Blackbourne. Save for occasionally serving her mistress, Emma, like Jeremy, had spent the day indolent.

Addison wondered if indentured servants ever received any compensation. Daliyah certainly deserved more than her peers for all the work she performed.

"While I appreciate Lord Blackbourne for allowing us to stay, it is dreadfully boring here," Jeremy said as he slumped in his chair.

"Indeed," Emma seconded. "What do you do for merriment, Mr. Brooke?"

"Very little," Addison replied. "The work here keeps me busy."

"It is a shame you cannot venture into town

in the evenings because of the wolves. Has Lord Blackbourne not considered living elsewhere?"

"How does he not die of boredom?" Jeremy asked.

"He has his books and enjoys riding and hunting," Mr. Brooke answered.

"What of his interest in finding a wife?" Emma inquired. "Surely he wants an heir?"

"Men of the aristocracy have the luxury of waiting," Jeremy said.

Having scarfed down his food, Addison rose to assist Miss Daliyah.

"You can leave her to it," Emma said. "She'll do a decent job of the cleaning, and she be grateful for it. Her lot in life could be far worse."

Addison wanted to respond that he was not so lazy that he could not lend a hand, but he would not offend Emma or Jeremy. He needed them to stay at Blackbourne for as long as possible.

Miss Daliyah had not looked up from where she washed the dishes, but she had surely heard everything they said.

He walked over to her. "May I join you?"

She looked up at him in surprise, perhaps wondering that he should even ask such a question. "If it is what you wish."

He smiled at her. "Are you always so agreeable?"

"I think there is not much to be gained by being disagreeable, sir."

Grabbing linen, he dried the dishes she washed. From the corners of his eyes, he saw Emma regarding them with a touch of envy, perhaps reconsidering whether or not to help in the cleaning. But she remained at the table with Jeremy as the two of them exchanged complaints about the weather, of Mr. Phillips delaying their departure, and how much better London would be.

Jeremy announced that, having nothing better to do, he would retire for the night. Miss Daliyah took the tea and milk she had prepared to her mistress.

Emma sidled up to Addison when they were the only two left in the kitchen. "Shall I expect you in my room tonight?"

Addison hesitated. The carnal in him wanted very much to answer in the affirmative, even though he did not find Emma nearly as comely as he had yesterday. He thought of Montague, but perhaps his brother would understand.

"I should like nothing more," Addison answered, "and only hope that I do not fall asleep too soon. I slept rather poorly last night and am rather weary from the day's work."

"If you are asleep, I will come wake you, shall I?"

To his surprise, he found himself wondering if Miss Daliyah would be receptive to his attentions. She was certainly not adverse to his company, nor impervious to his presence. Standing beside her as they washed and dried the dishes, he had seen her blush when his hand had grazed hers. She was less garrulous, but perhaps she felt less comfortable conversing with Emma and Jeremy present.

If Miss Daliyah were to welcome him into her bed, he would not likely hesitate.

"Or perhaps we should be cautious?" he said to Emma. "I would not wish to cause you to lose your employment with Miss Cameron."

"But how would she know?" Emma countered. "There are but the four of us in the servants' quarters, and Jeremy would not dare snitch on me for I know all his misdeeds."

"And Miss Daliyah?"

"If it were her word against mine, Miss

Cameron would never believe her."

"Why not?"

Emma blinked several times in surprise. "Surely you understand?"

"Miss Daliyah seems to possess a sincere nature."

Her eyes grew large. "She has pulled the wool over your eyes then, Mr. Brooke! She can be quite deceptive."

He could not believe it true, but he saw arguing with Emma would serve little use. "As regards the invitation tonight," he said, "I hesitate to compromise you a second time."

"But the deed be done. A second time would make no difference."

"We should not tempt Fate again so soon."

Emma furrowed her brow.

"I should not risk the ire of Lord Blackbourne," Addison added. "He seems taken by your mistress and would be appalled if he found my behavior wanting."

"Very well," Emma sighed. "But should you change your mind, I should not be bothered if you were to wake me."

Addison bowed and headed upstairs to see if Montague required his services. In the corridor, he came across Miss Daliyah standing before the door to the dungeon. Her presence there puzzled him, as it seemed she had not favored her earlier experience with it.

His approach startled her.

"The skeletons below...they met a horrid or unjust death," she remarked.

"I know not," he answered quickly. "I know little of the history of the castle, though it were possible they were imprisoned for sound reasons."

Looking down in thought, she seemed to doubt his word. But she had no cause to, and Addison deduced it was likely his guilty conscience that colored his perception.

"Regardless, it is not a happy place," he said, taking her by the elbow to lead her along.

"They looked as if in distress."

"They all do. Have you known skeletons to look at peace?" he snapped. By her reaction, he knew he had spoken too harshly. "Your pardon," he said. "I prefer to forget that part of the castle exists."

She nodded in understanding.

"I pray you have a more restful night tonight," he said as they stopped in front of her room.

"You as well."

As their gazes locked, he felt a strong desire to kiss her. How would those supple lips feel beneath his? How would her body feel in his arms?

He forced himself to give her a bow and wish her good night.

"Good night, Mr. Brooke," she returned before entering her room.

When she had closed the door behind her, he released a sigh. Perhaps he should not have been so hasty in refusing Emma's invitation.

Chapter Thirteen

"Save for Miss Daliyah, they all seem rather unconcerned about Mr. Phillips," Addison informed him.

Montague stared out his window. Though the clouds covered the moon at present, Montague could make out the tops of the trees. His eyesight at night, as well as his strength, had oddly improved since his transformation into a bloodthirsty demon.

"Miss Cameron as well," Montague said. "She seemed to almost welcome the extension of her stay. Her interest in me is plain."

"That is good. She had previously been in a hurry to reach London."

Montague walked over to where Addison

held a banyan and slid his arms into the sleeves. "It is no easy matter to be near her. Mr. Phillips was not sufficient enough to stay my hunger, and there is that *other* desire. I find myself trembling from it at times."

His brother looked down in thought before asking, "Have you gone through all of the books?"

"As before, there are no answers in any of them. The majority be pure rubbish, written to provoke more than inform, by men who have had suspect experiences. We have to find ourselves a true witch."

He sat down in a chair and sighed while Addison murmured the curse by memory.

"For your want of goodness and love," Addison said of the first line as he sat on the edge of a dresser. "Perhaps you are to fall in love with her?"

Montague groaned. "And how am I to achieve that?"

"Dwell upon her qualities."

"Such as?"

"She is beautiful."

"If that were the only quality needed, I should be in love with her already. All I want is

141

to sink my fangs into her and ravish her."

"She is charming," Addison provided.

"And dull. If I were not busy containing my lusts, I would have perished of her inane talk and gossip. I care not a pittance who was or was not received at court."

"Is she kind?"

"How the hell am I to know?"

"Does she support charities? Has she brothers or sisters who adore her?"

"She has two brothers of whom she speaks rather disparagingly and feels duty bound to rectify the damage they have done to the Cameron name. She also has an older sister, whom she accuses of jealousy and believes is doomed to spinsterhood because she has neither wits nor beauty."

Addison frowned. "Then you must find other qualities in her to love. And it might prove helpful to attempt to earn *her* love as well."

Again, Montague groaned. Even before the curse, he had not concerned himself with such unnecessary matters as love.

"As we have no clues as to what will lift the curse, we must attempt everything," Addison implored.

"Yes, yes," Montague grumbled.

"We have some time at our disposal."

"Do we?"

"On the morrow, I am to go into town in search of Mr. Phillips. Of course, I will not find him. Miss Cameron will have to stay another night. Perhaps several if it rains again and the road conditions are poor."

"And if it does not rain? At some point, she will want to hire another driver. And if she does not arrive in London, her family will certainly go in search of her."

Addison stood up and paced while he pondered. "You could suggest that she write a letter to her aunt in London telling of her delay."

"Yes, though she must not disclose that she is here at Blackbourne—quite inappropriately, as she is without family or a governess with her."

"But we should still have several days before her absence would cause concern. And it would cease to be inappropriate if you offered your hand in marriage."

"Would she accept?"

"You said her interest in you was plain."

"I suspect she is most interested in my title.

She is not the sort to live in a dark castle with but a handful of servants. And I cannot keep my appetites at bay. I wonder that I can even last this night."

Addison's features darkened. "Perhaps I can ask Miss Emma to accompany me into town. You could follow us into the woods and…"

Thinking about having to wait all those hours, Montague frowned. "And what would we tell Miss Cameron happened to her maid?"

"She was abducted by highwaymen?"

"She may grow suspicious that two of her servants have disappeared."

"Have we another choice?"

"Miss Cameron prefers Miss Emma to the other. You should ask Miss Daliyah to join you into town."

Addison appeared troubled by the suggestion.

"You do not agree?" Montague asked.

Rubbing the back of his neck, Addison replied, "I am weary of Miss Emma's attentions."

"What, already? And she has lifted her skirts but once to you. How can you tire of her cunnie so easily?"

Addison shrugged. "We simply do not suit."

Montague narrowed his eyes. "Cunnie be cunnie."

"I beg to differ."

"Have you always been so particular?"

"Do you not notice? They all vary in size, shape, scent."

"I notice, especially the scent. But I *care* not. That is the difference."

"There is, too, the whole of the person."

Montague raised a brow. "The whole of the person? What the bloody hell has that to do with cunnie?"

"Suffice it to say Miss Emma's eagerness has dampened my ardor."

"I should never have thought to wish that I could experience the same," Montague sighed. "Alas, it seems my ardor will never let me have a moment's peace."

After Addison left, Montague remained in his chair and sat in the dark when the candles had burnt out, struggling with the desires that burned his body.

What if Addison was right? What if he had to fall in love with Miss Cameron? He would gladly offer his hand in matrimony. That was easy enough. He cared not whom he took for a wife, and he supposed one that was a delight to the eyes was better than any other. But love her? How long would that take? What if it never happened? What if she discovered what he really was?

Infuriated by questions without answers, Montague leaped to his feet. He wanted to howl in rage. It was as if Fate was toying with him, tempting him with this beauty, an antidote he could not consume. He wanted to tear apart his chambers. He wanted to feed. He needed release.

He would have it. Tonight. He could not wait till the morning.

But he did wait several hours till everyone was sound asleep. Then, quietly and with more calm deliberation than he felt, he descended the stairs into the servants' quarters. He knew not which room belonged to which servant, but he could smell the difference. Ever since the curse had made him a beast, his senses had been heightened, likely comparable to that of a dog.

He stopped in front of the door of the maid named Emma. Addison preferred this one less, but Miss Cameron clearly thought Emma the superior servant. Despite his own preferences, Addison would be less likely to be devastated at the loss of his preferred maid than Miss Cameron would over hers.

Thus, Montague moved to the room of the one named Daliyah. Remembering her sweet scent, he inhaled deeply. His body throbbed in anticipation. His fangs emerged. He salivated.

Carefully, he opened the door and was greeted by her soft breathing and the faint light of the moon, momentarily between clouds, coming in through the small window. With light steps, he approached her bed. She stirred, and her lashes fluttered.

Before she opened her eyes, he was upon her, covering her mouth.

Her lashes flew open, her eyes widening in surprise, then alarm, just as he sank his fangs into her neck.

'Sblood, she tasted sweet.

She screamed into his hand and struggled, but even had he his former, inferior strength, she wouldn't have been able to throw him off. The squirming of her body beneath him sent his lust ablaze.

He waited for his venom to take over. Soon

enough, her struggling slowed. Her cries turned into moans.

He pried himself from her neck before draining her life. He had no interest in ravishing a corpse and usually finished feeding after he had satiated his carnal appetite.

When she ceased struggling and her hips pressed upward against him, not to push him away but to invite him closer, he unbuttoned his fall, then yanked the blanket from her. His head swam with the scent of her, the feel of her, the taste of her, all conspiring to burst his cods and boil his blood.

Pulling up her shift, he reached for her thighs to push them apart. How did she have such smooth legs? Looking into her countenance, he saw the familiar glazed expression of all his prey. Half drained of life, intoxicated with arousal, they capitulated to their own demise.

Sliding his hand to her quim, he felt dampness, an effect of the venom. She was ready to be taken.

Unable to wait any longer, he shoved himself into her.

'Sblood!

There was naught more magnificent than the embrace of cunnie about his cock. His member pulsed in the glory of her wet heat. He pushed himself farther. It seemed her hips rose to meet his thrusts. He went deeper. And deeper. And deeper still, as if he wanted to shove all of himself inside her.

What was this euphoria he found himself drowning in? He felt warmth spreading from his cock to his belly, his bosom, his arms and legs, every part of him. He had never felt its like before.

He glanced at her face, but she stared at nothing. Her lips were parted, allowing soft, husky moans to escape.

As he continued to thrust into her, the sensations increased. Rather than tearing into her cunnie in his urgency to quench the flame, he found himself reveling in the bliss, building his crescendo gradually. Her cunnie grew warmer and wetter, aiding his ascent. He felt her ripple along his member. There were times when his prey would spend, a final gift before they died.

With a groan, he delved into her glory. The swell of ardor in his cods passed into his cock, which released its fluid form into her waiting heat. He pumped his hips even after he had drained himself, seeking to prolong the ecstasy. He shuddered from head to toe and eventually collapsed atop her.

Soaked in rapture, he had forgotten to sink his fangs back into her just before he climaxed. The combination of feeding and spending at the same time was exquisite. Seeing the small rivulet of blood upon her neck reminded him of this.

Lowering his head toward her, he bared his fangs.

Chapter Fourteen

Addison brushed his lips over hers as he rolled his hips, diving himself deeper into her. She wrapped her arms around his neck. Her moans grew in urgency. He thrust against her narrow hips. She started to gasp. Holding back his torrent of desire, he bucked until she, with a cry, reached her peak. He took his turn shortly after, quickening his thrusts till he grunted with relief.

Withdrawing from Miss Emma, he rolled onto his back. She curled closer to him. Lying beside her in his bed, he stared up at the ceiling. He had not intended to bed her tonight, but when he had not appeared in her room, she'd come to his.

She had wanted to lay with him again, and Addison found a tiny morsel of solace in granting her what may prove to be her final wish. In truth, even if tomorrow were not her last, he would have found it difficult to refuse her advances. But even as he fucked her, his mind was elsewhere. He wondered if Miss Daliyah would ever consider lifting her skirts beneath him?

After several minutes, he turned to Miss Emma. "We had best return you to your room."

"Must we?" she murmured, nestling even closer.

"It would not be seemly for you to be seen leaving my room in the morning."

"No one but Jeremy or Daliyah would see, and as I've said, they will not tell."

Not eager to spend the night with Miss Emma in his bed, Addison persisted. "I have to rise early in the morning. I would disturb your sleep. And as I am unaccustomed to having company in my bed, I think I should sleep more soundly were I by myself."

He got up, pulled up his breeches, and held his hand out to her. With a sigh, she allowed him to help her to her feet. Taking the candle, he walked her back to her room before returning to his, where he sat down on his bed but felt little desire to sleep.

Though he had limited fondness for Miss Emma, he mourned her coming demise. He dreaded the morning, when he would have to ask her to accompany him into town. She would, of course, accept. They would take the curricle, on the pretense that they might be bringing back Mr. Phillips. Montague would follow behind.

Addison dreaded the screams that would ring in his ears as she fought against Montague. The screams would eventually turn to lustful moans as she succumbed to his ardor, her body a willing victim to its own rape. Then there would be silence as her life drained from her, leaving her body ashen and crumpled.

Addison silenced an anguished cry. He wanted to lash out at every object in his room but dared not wake the others. Though his tears had run dry long ago, the remorse and guilt always dragged him into his personal hell. He had thought, at one point, to put them both out of their miseries. Montague owned a fine pair of pistols and had once gifted Addison his own pair. After loading the firearm with powder and bullet, he had intended to shoot first Montague and then himself.

But in the end, he had been unable to pull the trigger. Montague had no wish to die, and Addison had not the fortitude to murder his own brother. As youths, it was Montague who had wiped Addison's tears after he had fallen from a horse; Montague who had taught him how to read, shoot, and play cricket; and Montague who never failed to share his biscuits and confections with Addison. The fourth Earl of Blackbourne had fathered Addison, but it was Montague who filled the parental role.

His candle eventually burnt down, but Addison continued to sit in the dark, shoulders hunched in defeat, as if by staying up, he could delay the morning.

Only when he heard footsteps in the corridor did he lift his head. Had he heard correctly? It was doubtful anyone would be awake at this time. But he had thought the same of the previous night, till Miss Daliyah had surprised him by being awake. Was it her again? Perhaps what she had seen down in the dungeon haunted her. Perhaps she'd had a nightmare.

Rising to his feet, he lit his candle and opened his bedroom door and looked into the corridor. He saw no one. He had been mistaken. Perhaps he had heard a mouse.

Without bothering to remove his waistcoat or breeches, he lay down on his bed. He had ceased praying long ago, but tonight he closed his eyes and prayed for the salvation that may have finally appeared to come their way. The sooner they discerned how Miss Cameron might break the curse, the more lives would be spared. Miss Emma's death would be hard to bear, but he would be more pained to lose Miss Daliyah. He thought about trying to convince Montague to take Jeremy instead, but that would only delay the inevitable.

Addison fisted his hand and slammed the side of it against the wall. Several months into the curse, Montague, seeing the pain it caused Addison, had told him to leave. But Addison could not abandon his brother to endure the curse alone. And so it had ensnared the both of them.

Hearing a gasp, Addison sat up.

The sound had been faint, and he wondered if he heard correctly. He had not closed his door fully.

Then he heard a moan.

Getting up, he stepped into the corridor. He heard a rustling sound. It was coming from Miss Daliyah's room. Walking over, he put his ear to her door—and heard the familiar sounds of rutting.

Montague!

Pushing the door open, he stepped in and saw his brother over Miss Daliyah, lowering his mouth toward her neck.

Striding over, Addison grabbed Montague and pulled him off of her.

"You said you would refrain!" he exclaimed in a harsh whisper.

"I tried," Montague replied.

With a curse, Addison went to Miss Daliyah. She looked pale to him. But he saw her bosom rise and fall.

"She's still alive," he remarked.

"I did not finish feeding upon her, though by God, I've never tasted blood as sweet."

Addison refrained from glaring at his brother and remained fixed upon Miss Daliyah. He took her hand. It was still warm to the touch. There was hope.

"And when I was inside her," Montague continued, buttoning his fall, "it was...it was glorious."

Addison cursed again. He had no interest in hearing Montague speak of this. He wanted only to know how he might ensure Miss Daliyah survived.

"Unlike anything I've ever felt," Montague marveled.

"I think we cannot leave her here," Addison considered aloud. "If she should improve, she might accuse you of attacking her."

"Would anyone believe her? I would, of course, deny any such thing."

"Still, do we wish to risk suspicion?"

"Then perhaps I should finish feeding. Though...I feel quite satisfied."

Surprised, Addison studied his brother, who had always complained that feeding only resolved the majority of his hunger. It never did away with the whole of his cravings. Montague appeared equally perplexed by his unusual state.

"I will move her, away from the others," Addison decided.

"To the dungeon?"

Miss Daliyah had already had an uncomfortable brush with that place.

"The bedchamber in the East Tower," Addison said, scooping Miss Daliyah into his arms. "Take the candle from my room. I have not your ability to see in the dark."

Montague obliged before following Addison as he carried her upstairs.

"The tower chambers are fine rooms, reserved for guests of note," Montague said.

"No one will be able to hear her if she is in the tower."

"Would it not be easier if I simply finished feeding upon her, then you can dispose of her entirely?"

Addison said nothing.

They walked in silence until Montague said, "You are partial to her."

"You as well," Addison returned. "I thought we had agreed you would take Miss Emma in the morning."

"I could not wait till morning, and Miss Cameron would be much less happy were she to lose that maid. And as you were busy fucking Miss Emma, I thought to find myself available cunnie."

Addison paused.

"You think I could not smell your activity?" Montague asked.

Without responding, Addison continued walking. They made their way into the tower. The key to the bedchamber hung beside the door. Montague opened it.

"Take her while I adjust the bedclothes," Addison said.

Montague appeared taken aback at receiving yet another order from Addison, who always knew his place despite their relation, but made no objection as he received Miss Daliyah into his arms.

After pulling aside the covers, Addison took her weak and prone form and laid her upon the bed. He covered her with the bedclothes. She continued to stare at nothing. Her lips trembled. Addison felt her forehead and found it cool and damp.

"Damnation," he cursed.

Looking about, he decided to start a fire in the hearth.

Montague watched without word before finally saying, "Such effort on behalf of a—"

Ignoring the comment, Addison said, "We

should agree on what to say to the others. We could say she took ill."

"If that is what you wish."

"It will do for now."

"And what is it you intend with Miss Daliyah?"

To keep her alive if I can, Addison silently replied. He met his brother's gaze. "You seemed to find her cunnie exceptional. Perhaps I wish for a taste myself."

Chapter Fifteen

Back in his own chambers, Montague shook his head. How could his brother have taken a fancy to that dressing maid? Granted, Montague had, at first, found her features too unfamiliar to deem her comely, but after much study, Montague decided she was more attractive than the other maid. Nevertheless, Miss Daliyah was hardly worthy of much notice.

And yet she had felt divine. But he supposed the most rancid of waters would taste heavenly after a drought, and he had been famished for flesh.

As he went to bed, he continued to wonder at the magnificence of his climax, at how gratified he felt in both his appetites. Surely this momentary satiety would disappear by morning, but he slept more soundly than he had in years.

To his surprise, when he woke, his thirst for blood and flesh had not yet returned.

He rang for Addison, who took some time in appearing.

"I had not thought you to be awake in the early hours of the morning," his brother explained when he finally arrived after Montague had rung for him thrice.

Montague drew aside the curtains to look outside. There were fewer clouds than the night before, but the brightness of day did not trouble him as much today.

"Nevertheless, where were you?" he asked of Addison.

"Tending to Miss Daliyah. I thought she might be in a panic if she woke to find herself in an unfamiliar setting." Addison studied him closer. "You look well, my brother."

"I *feel* well...invigorated, even."

Addison prepared the articles for his shave. "Indeed?"

"It is a relief not to be tormented by hunger

or burning with lust."

"That is truly wondrous."

Montague sat down and allowed Addison to place linen over his shirt and about his shoulders. "I have not felt the like—not even for a second—since the day I was cursed."

"Is it the presence of Miss Cameron, you think?"

"It is possible. Or perhaps the blood of the maid holds properties that suit my hunger."

"How could that be? You have fed on all manner of men and women. Did they not all taste the same?"

"They did," Montague acknowledged.

"The curse made no mention of rare blood."

"The words do point to Miss Cameron."

"Then you have but to marry her to keep her forever in your company," Addison said.

Montague sighed at the prospect of so easy an antidote. His spirits, which had wallowed in the depths of despair for so long, finally began to surface.

"I will relish my current state, but it is too early for false hope," he tempered.

Addison nodded. "That is wise. Do you still wish for me to ask Miss Emma to accompany me into town, then?"

"I think not. I do not wish to distress Miss Cameron, as she has already lost one maid to illness. I take it you locked the room Miss Daliyah is in?"

"I did. I wish I did not have to go into town in search of Mr. Phillips. If Miss Daliyah wakes…"

"If she does, what do you fear?"

"She would be startled to find herself in a strange place."

"You want I should look in on her?"

Addison said nothing.

"You do not trust me," Montague deduced.

"What if your hunger returns?"

Montague pressed his lips into a grim line. "You must shed this fancy for her. If, as you wonder, my hunger returns, her fate is sealed."

Addison sighed and, undoubtedly seeing the wisdom presented by his older brother, nodded in understanding.

"What is it about her that draws you?" Montague asked as Addison finished with the shave.

"She is kind and possesses an impressive forbearance."

"Perhaps that is the lot of indentured servants. Their liberties are limited till the end of their indenture."

"It is more than that."

"You have not come across many indentured servants. They are less common in England than in the colonies. You would not know if her qualities are natural or more the result of her circumstances."

Addison was silent, but Montague sensed it was not from agreement.

"If your hunger returns while I am gone," Addison said after he had finished assisting Montague with his wardrobe, "will you promise to refrain from addressing it till I am returned?"

Montague frowned. "For what purpose? You wish to sample Miss Daliyah's cunnie before I drain her life?"

"Perhaps."

"Then ravish her now, before you leave for town."

"I have a great many chores to attend to, including breakfast for Miss Cameron when she wakes."

Montague released a sigh. "Very well, I will refrain, but do not be too long in town."

"You said last night that you would refrain," Addison said with a wry curl of his lips.

"I swear I will attempt my best."

"Perhaps the more time you spend with Miss Cameron, the greater her effect upon you."

Montague considered the possibility. "Yes, though I fear she will soon exhaust all topics at her disposal."

"You could go riding with her."

"A capital idea. Surely she will not feel the need to talk as much then."

Montague decided to take breakfast with Miss Cameron. He even allowed the curtains to be drawn aside to let in the late-morning light.

"Mr. Brooke will be going into town to determine the whereabouts of Mr. Phillips and to procure fresh bread and meats," Montague informed her after watching her poke with disinterest at her boiled eggs.

"Would the town have Bath Cakes, you think?" Miss Cameron asked. "They are perhaps my favorite pastries."

Montague could not remember the taste of the buns decorated with carraway comfits, but then, he had only cared for the taste of blood these past several years. "I will certainly ask it of Mr. Brooke," Montague replied. "What else do you favor?"

"At home, I always have chocolate for breakfast."

"I will have Mr. Brooke procure some cocoa, then."

Miss Cameron smiled. "Your kindness brightens my day! I must confess I am rather out of sorts this morning, as my maid Emma cannot find Daliyah. Emma and I were quite put out that we had not her assistance with my toilette. It is quite careless, selfish even, of Daliyah to neglect her duties in this manner. But this is what comes when one is not stern enough with servants like her. They are too stupid to remember how they must act and must be upbraided constantly."

"I fear I have caused you distress. I should have come to you earlier to explain that Miss Daliyah has taken ill. My man, Addison, discovered her feverish and moved her to a different room, should her ailment prove contagious."

"Ah. Feverish you say?"

"And delirious. I can send for a doctor if you wish, though fevers can resolve themselves."

"I should not wish to trouble you."

"It were no trouble at all to be of service to you."

She smiled, and after he proposed a ride to enjoy the respite from the rain, she brightened even more.

Once they had set out on their steeds, for the first time in many years, Montague relished the fresh air, the wind as it passed through his hair, and the thrill of putting his horse into full gallop. He felt human.

Moreover, since it seemed Miss Cameron was already having a positive effect upon the curse, he did not mind her company as much as he had before.

When he and Miss Cameron returned to the castle, Addison had not yet returned from town. Montague sat in his riding clothes for half an hour, reflecting upon his good fortune that the answer to his prayers had landed in his lap so easily.

Upon his return, Addison went straightway to Miss Daliyah's room before coming down to assist Montague with removing his riding boots.

"How does she fare?" Montague asked.

Addison shook his head. "Asleep and no

different from last night. Did she stir when I was gone?"

"I know not. I did not attend to her. Miss Cameron and I went for a ride. I had forgotten how much I enjoy riding."

"You seem in good spirits."

"In truth, I feel like a new man."

"I am glad to hear it," said Addison, emotion filling his countenance. "Have your appetites returned?"

"Not as of yet."

"This is all quite promising."

"Aye. After years of damnation, I may finally be rid of this curse."

Prior to dinner, Addison made a report of his findings before Montague and Miss Cameron. He found no one in town who had seen Mr. Phillips.

Miss Cameron inquired, "Now what are we to do?"

"We could put together a search party," Montague suggested.

She turned to him. "You would do this? Once again, your benevolence impresses me, my lord!"

Between having to attend to the guests, his

customary chores, and looking in on Miss Daliyah, Addison appeared busier than he had ever been. Before they each retired for the night, he told Montague that Miss Daliyah would at times open her eyes, but her periods of wakefulness did not last but a few minutes.

"I think I will stay by her side through the night, should she wake and require assistance," Addison said.

Montague stared at his brother. "You are more partial to this maid than I thought. I would not have guessed it, though her blood and cunnie were exceptionally sweet. But you will have to set aside your attentions toward her. Tomorrow you will have to return to town to assemble a search party. I think three days should constitute a sufficient period of time before we have to conclude the worst to Miss Cameron."

The following morning, to his relief, his body still felt at peace. He spent as much time with Miss Cameron as he could. The rain clouds remained at bay, and they went riding once more. They had tea upon a veranda and even played a round of pall-mall before the clouds darkened.

"I think I shall never master this game!" Miss Cameron lamented when her wooden ball stopped well short of the iron hoop.

Montague took his turn and sent his ball through.

Miss Cameron applauded. "I would I had your skills!"

"I fancy it luck," he mused, "for I have not played in several years."

"One would not know it given how well you have struck your balls."

She took a weak swing. The ball rolled several feet and remained short of the hoop.

"I think you would fare better if you employed your wrists less and swung with more of your arms," he advised.

She gave him a quizzical look. He demonstrated how she tended to swing, then showed her the larger arc of his swing. She attempted to copy his swing but with limited success.

"May I?" he asked.

"You may," she replied with a subtly flirtatious smile.

He wrapped his arms about her and placed his hands over hers. The scent of her perfume overwhelmed his nose, and he wanted to withdraw, but he forced himself to stay. "Keep your wrists and arms stiff. Imagine the mallet as an extension of your arms."

He swung her arms with his. The mallet struck the ball, which went several yards past its target. Miss Cameron gasped with pleasure. She turned her head toward him, and wisps of her hair brushed against his cheek.

"You are an exceptional instructor, my lord," she said, her voice husky and low.

"And you an apt pupil," he returned, gazing into her eyes of cerulean blue. "Forgive my impertinence, but would my efforts warrant a kiss as a reward?"

Her eyes glimmered. "If you deem it so, my lord."

He cupped her chin in one hand and, tilting her mouth upward, covered her lips with his. She tasted bland, but her lips were soft to the touch. When their mouths parted, she appeared more than willing to continue the kiss.

"Your pardon," he said. "I should not take such liberties. You are without protection and a guest under my roof, but I must admit the thought of a kiss has been upon my mind since morning."

She grinned. "Has it?"

"Miss Cameron, I have shunned the company of others for a long time, but since Providence saw fit to have you cross my threshold, I realize what I have been missing. I want nothing more than to assist you in your journey, and yet, selfishly, I savor your delay, as it means I can be longer in your company."

She glowed at his words and murmured, "I have thought it Providence as well."

"Though we have known each other but for a short time, my sentiments are strong. It is as if the hand of Destiny were at work."

She looked about to melt. "I could not agree more."

"In truth, I would I could keep you here forever."

Her smile broadened. "You must come to London, where we can begin a proper courtship."

Wrapping an arm about her waist, he pulled her close to him. "I doubt I can wait the length of a proper courtship."

She let out a breathless giggle. "Nor can I. But my father will not arrive in London till at least a fortnight hence. He could not fail to be impressed by you. I am certain he would approve."

"I pray you are right," he said, brushing his lips over hers before claiming her mouth.

She sighed against him, and they parted only because they heard the rumble of thunder. Montague suggested they continue the croquet the following day.

"Only if you will assist and provide instruction once more," Miss Cameron said with sly smile.

"But of course," Montague replied with a bow.

Once inside, Miss Cameron wanted to change for the evening. Montague retired to his chambers, satisfied with how quickly and easily Miss Cameron fell into his plans. If her father was as agreeable as she, they could be wed within a month or two.

But his state of bliss and hope suffered a setback in the evening. Despite the hours he had spent with her that day, by evening, the tentacles of his previous appetites threatened to return.

Chapter Sixteen

Shadows danced across the room. At times, Daliyah feared they would attack her, as *that* one had, and she could not fend them off, for her body felt drained of its strength. As a child, she'd had scarlet fever and remembered lying in bed, too fatigued to move. But instead of a fever, this time she felt cold, even beneath the bedclothes and with a fire burning in the room.

A fire? How was there a fire in a servant's chamber?

But she did not attempt to answer the query and instead closed her eyes and drifted back into sleep.

When she awoke, she grew cognizant of a rawness between her legs, of moisture there. She recalled a surge of ardor in her dreams, not felt since her days with Isaiah, followed by smarting, of flesh tearing into flesh. But her body had welcomed it, had wanted more. It had seemed real, but it must have been a dream.

She fell asleep before she could contemplate more.

When she opened her eyes next, she thought she saw Mr. Brooke standing at her bedside. He took her hand and pressed it in his. What was happening? Was she dreaming? Where was she? The room looked different. She *was* dreaming then.

Her next dream turned into a nightmare. The skeletons from the dungeon hissed at her. *Flee*, they said. *You must flee.*

And she did. Into the woods. However, the wolves were there, waiting for her. She had no choice but to return to the castle. But as she reached the gates, a large shadow leaped toward her.

Her eyes flew open, but no dark and ominous presence threatened her. Her heart still raced, but she realized she had been dreaming. She was not out in the woods but in the comfort of her room—nay, a room. And not far from her, Mr. Brooke sat in a chair, slumped over in slumber. She stirred, causing him to wake.

He was upon his feet and beside the bed in an instant. "Miss Daliyah?"

"Where...?" she began. Her mouth felt dry and her body weak.

Looking relieved that she could speak, he asked if she wanted something to drink.

She nodded.

He walked over to the fireplace, where a kettle hung. With the hot water, he made her tea. When she struggled to sit, he assisted her and moved several pillows behind her. She looked down upon the silken bedclothes. This was assuredly not quarters for a servant. Why had she been moved?

Gratefully, she took the cup of tea from him and took a small sip as the contents were quite hot.

"Thank you," she said in a small voice. Looking about once more, she noted the gilded furnishings with ornate details in the Chippendale style: an armoire, a sideboard, a table flanked by a pair of Queen Anne chairs. Unlike the window in her room, the one in her present chambers was large and finished with velvet curtains complete with silken tassels.

She turned to Mr. Brooke, whose gaze seemed not to have left her. "How...?"

"You fell ill," he explained. "I thought you might be more comfortable in a different room."

"That were...kind, Mr. Brooke."

"Pray, do not expend your energy in talk, lest you require something of me."

She took another sip of tea, then felt too fatigued to finish the rest. She attempted to place it on the bedside table but needed the assistance of Mr. Brooke.

"I should... Miss Cameron will..." she tried. Her mistress would not be pleased to have her ill and indisposed.

"Worry not," Mr. Brooke assured her. "Emma and I will attend to whatever your mistress needs. You need only rest and recover."

She thought to protest, but her eyelids grew heavy. Closing her eyes, she went back to sleep.

She woke to find Mr. Brooke gone. She recalled how she had found him asleep in a chair. How long had he sat with her? She looked about the room once more and saw that a fresh cup of tea along with a plate of bread and cheese had been placed on the bedside table. Such a thoughtful man was Mr. Brooke!

Had she been cognizant of being moved, she would have protested. In truth, she was a little surprised that Miss Cameron would have allowed her to be moved into such fine quarters. She wondered how Mr. Brooke had managed to convince her mistress and Lord Blackbourne. Or perhaps he had not and had simply moved her without their permission.

She was glad, though, to be out of her previous accommodations. A part of her wanted never to return to the room. Evil had lurked there. Evil mixed with lust. How strange it had been to go from fear to desire. Only dreams were possessed of such little sense. Yet it had all felt too vivid to be a dream. There was even a faint soreness between her legs.

But if the assault had been real, her body would not have filled with desire. Thus, it had to have been a dream, a strange and striking dream, perhaps brought on by her sudden and mysterious malaise.

She reached for the cup of tea. The contents

were tepid, but she drank it all. She even broke off some of the bread. How had she become ill? Were others sick as well? This illness was not one familiar to her. She felt drained of strength but had no other symptoms: no fever, headaches, or abdominal pains.

She partook of the cheese. Cheese was not a favorite of hers as it sometimes upset her stomach, but she was hungry. What she truly desired was beefsteak, thick and juicy. Her mouth watered at the thought of the moisture dripping from the pink flesh. She had tasted of beefsteak but twice in her life, back in Barbados. Once, the cook had sliced off a small bite for her to sample when she was a child. She was six and ten the second time. Waiting to clear the table for her father, he had noticed her staring at the remains on his plate. Declaring himself "stuffed to the gills," he had said she could dispose of his plate however she wished. She had brought it back to the kitchen to share with the others.

Daliyah wondered how long she had slept. A day? Two? Regardless of the duration, Miss Cameron would be displeased. Emma too. Especially if Mr. Phillips had returned. Daliyah hoped her illness had not delayed their departure for too long. She also hoped Mr. Phillips had indeed returned. Since arriving at Castle Blackbourne, her nerves had been on edge. Venturing into the dungeon had only made matters worse. Could that have caused her illness? The air down there had certainly seemed ominous. Could dreams make one ill?

More alert now, she recalled the dream from beginning to end. It had started with a hand or object clamped over her mouth, stifling her cries of surprise. Then came a piercing sensation near the back of her neck. Next, a warmth spread through her. She struggled to dislodge the weight pressing down upon her body till desire filled her veins and ardor pooled between her legs. Her initial panic faded. She found herself lifting her hips toward her assailant. His hardness pressed against her, and she ached for him. At the time, she had not asked herself how it was possible. Only in her dreams could she crave to be ravished by a man she could not know or see.

When his member had pierced her, she had welcomed the fullness between her legs. Divine agitation waved through her with each of his thrusts, sending her body to the pinnacle of carnal pleasure. Its beautiful radiance outshone the sting in her neck. She felt *his* euphoria as well, and heard his sigh before he was torn from her.

Remembering the bliss that had flooded her body during the dream, Daliyah grew warm and felt her cunnie pulse. Wanting to turn her mind to something else, she brushed her fingers through the tangles in her hair. When her hand brushed against her neck, she felt two raw scars, corresponding to where she felt she had been pierced in the dream.

How was that possible?

Chapter Seventeen

Daliyah heard footsteps, and the door to the bedchamber opened soon after.

"Miss Daliyah," Mr. Brooke greeted. "You look better."

"I feel better," she replied.

Looking over at her bedside table, he must have noticed she had partaken of what he had left. "Would you care for more bread and cheese? Or perhaps some biscuits?"

"You are too kind, Mr. Brooke," she protested.

"What may I bring you?"

Never having been waited on before save by her grandmother, she felt flustered. "Truly, I require nothing save perhaps my garments."

"I placed them in the armoire."

"Then I should dress and attend to Miss Cameron."

He shook his head. "You are to rest until you are fully well."

"But Miss Cameron—"

"She has agreed to Lord Blackbourne's directive."

"His lordship wants for me to remain here?"

"He, er, feels responsible that you fell ill under his roof. He has even offered to hire another maid if Miss Cameron truly needs more than one."

"How generous of him!" Lord Blackbourne had not struck her as the benevolent sort, but he likely wanted to impress Miss Cameron. "Nevertheless, I should inform them that I am on the mend," she said.

"I will convey the happy news to them." He went to stoke the fire.

"I have been an imposition to everyone, and especially you," she said.

He turned to her. "Not at all."

"But you must have more important matters to attend."

"I am happy to be of service to you, Miss Daliyah."

She stared at him. He sounded sincere. And though she had known him for but a few days, it did not surprise her that he, of all the servants, was caring for her.

"Mr. Brooke, I could not be more grateful for your kindness. I should like to return the favor. Perhaps there is some mending or sewing I can do for you?"

"Your health is sufficient compensation."

He poured her a fresh cup of tea, which she accepted.

"I wonder what manner of illness overcame me?" she thought aloud. "It came of a sudden."

"Perhaps a fever, mayhap influenza."

"It induced the strangest of dreams."

"Indeed?"

"I dreamt someone came into my room and...and I was bitten, I think."

She felt the back of her neck again. Mr. Brooke seemed to shift in discomfort.

"Perhaps a vicious spider caused my illness?" she inquired.

"That is quite possible. I will fetch you some biscuits. I insist."

After Mr. Brooke had left and she finished her tea, she got out of bed and went to stand before a looking glass near the fireplace in an attempt to look at the wound on her neck. She saw what looked to be two puncture marks. They were far too visible and rather large for a spider bite. But what else could possibly have bitten her? A rodent? Perhaps the spider had bitten her twice?

The door opened again, and Mr. Brooke appeared with a tray of biscuits and milk. His gaze traveled briefly down her body, and she realized that, silhouetted against the fire, her form must show through her thin chemise. She flushed and went back to the bed.

He set the tray beside her. "I thought you might like some milk with your tea."

She looked at him with wonder and gratitude. "Thank you, Mr. Brooke. I've not known more kindness since coming to England."

"I am sorry to hear it, for what I do is nothing exceptional."

"It *is* exceptional."

He poured tea and milk into a cup for her. "I fear England has been unkind to you."

"In England, I have not had to hear or

witness the horrors that are a near daily occurrence in Barbados." It was one of the reasons she had taken the extraordinary step of becoming an indentured servant.

"Your pardon. I did not mean to bring up painful memories for you."

Not wanting to dwell on the past, she said, "I think I am well enough to dress and attend to Miss Cameron."

"Miss Emma assists your mistress, and as she will retire soon for the night, there is little to be done."

"Is the hour so late, then?"

"Aye."

"How long have I been ill?"

"Two days."

"Two days!" She shook her head in amazement. "Well, for certain I shall resume my duties in the morning."

"I pray you have a good night's rest, free of unsettling dreams."

"Yes. Do you...do you have a great many dreams here at Castle Blackbourne?"

He looked down. "I used to."

"But no longer?"

"On occasion. Are you fearful of having

another dream?" he asked, as his gaze seemed to search the depths of hers.

"A little."

"In your dream, who entered your quarters?"

"I could not tell. A dark and heavy form. I think it a man, yet he was not merely a man."

"And what did he do?"

She hesitated. "He came upon me and...and bit me. But I realize now it was the bite of some creature that infiltrated my dream."

"Do you remember anything else?"

Not wanting to divulge her body's unexpected response to the assault, she shook her head.

"Do you pray, Miss Daliyah?" Mr. Brooke asked.

"I do."

"Perhaps an additional prayer or two may keep the frightful dream away."

He spoke in eerie earnest. After he had bid her good night and departed, she rose from the bed to use the chamber pot. She would dispose of the contents herself in the morning, for surely even Mr. Brooke had his limits.

She settled back into the bed, marveling at its luxury. Having slept for the better part of two days, sleep now eluded her. She stared at the fire and recounted all her moments with Mr. Brooke. She would miss him when they departed. Despite the palpable affinity they had in each other, naught could come of it. But she would forever cherish his kindness, a reminder that not all humanity was bad.

Several hours went by. The rain outside grew louder, drowning out the dying crackling of the embers in the hearth.

The sound of footsteps drew her from her reverie. Was it Mr. Brooke? But he had no reason to pay her a visit in the middle of the night.

Sitting up, she tightened her grip upon the bedclothes. The footsteps had stopped in front of her door. The handle of the door rattled, and her heart leaped into her throat.

Was it the shadow from her dream? She looked about for a weapon, though she feared the sound of her movement might confirm her presence. She would rather whatever lurked outside her door to decide no one was here.

Or perhaps it was Emma come to scold her? Or Jeremy to scare her, as he had done with the dungeon?

Despite those plausible and calming thoughts, her heart continued to beat rapidly. The door shook several times but must have been locked, for it did not open. Who had locked it? It was likely Mr. Brooke...but why would he have done so?

After another try, whoever stood on the other side of the door seemed to retreat. The footsteps faded away. Daliyah released a breath of relief after it seemed the intended intruder would not return.

Nevertheless, she went over and grabbed the poker from the fireplace, intending to keep it by her bedside the rest of the night.

Chapter Eighteen

The following morning, Addison went to Miss Daliyah's room when she rang. When he unlocked her door and entered, he found she had dressed herself.

"I rang because I knew not how to leave," she explained to him. "The door was locked."

"Your pardon," he said, glad to see that she looked to be in full health. "I have a habit of keeping this room locked."

She tilted her head, likely wondering why he would need the room locked when there was but him and Montague in the castle, but she knew it was none of her business and did not pry.

"I pray you slept well last night?" he asked.

"I have slept far too much these past few

days," she replied, "but I was startled in the middle of the night by a shaking of the door. It was as if someone wanted entry."

He frowned. No one but Montague knew the room she presently occupied.

"Perhaps it was the wind?" he suggested. "I might have left a window open."

"I thought I heard footsteps."

"The echo in this castle can be quite the annoyance. I find sounds can reach me from the strangest places. Would you care for breakfast? I had boiled some eggs."

She nodded and went to retrieve her belongings from the armoire.

He stopped her. "There is no need. You have the use of his room for as long as you desire it."

Her eyes widened. "But...I could not..."

"His lordship insists."

Her bottom lip dropped. Addison understood her reaction. It was quite unusual for a servant to be granted such fine chambers, and Montague had not approved her continued use, but Addison cared not. She deserved the comforts after what she had suffered.

"I think my mistress would not approve," Miss Daliyah demurred.

"Then she will have to convince my master otherwise. Till then, these chambers are yours."

Taking the articles from her arms, he placed them back in the armoire. "Come, let us to breakfast."

She remained doubtful. "Are you quite certain his lordship wants me in these chambers? As much as I appreciate his kind gesture, I've no wish to upset my mistress."

She reached for her items once more, but he blocked her, and her hand landed upon his chest, near his heart. She stared at her hand, which seemed seared to him. Emotion surged through Addison. He clasped his hand over hers.

He wanted to tell Miss Daliyah her mistress be damned. Instead, he said, "It would please his lordship."

Her eyes, a contrast of dark and white, looked to be searching the depths of his. Her voice became a near whisper. "Would it?"

"It would."

She knew it was *he* who would be pleased. His gaze went from her eyes to her lips. He had never wanted to kiss a pair as much as he did now. He knew not how it had come to this, that he could be so drawn to her, and yet all others of her sex paled in comparison.

If he kissed her now, with or without her permission, he sensed that she would not recoil. Indeed, she wanted it as much as he. Her touch made him…glow. He was reminded of how she had calmed the injured horse with a simple touch.

But she must have realized that a kiss would be improper, for she pulled away. Reluctantly, he allowed her. She made no more protestations regarding her new quarters.

"I have, also, fresh bread I had purchased while in town," he said.

"Did you find Mr. Phillips?" she asked as she followed him down the winding stairs of the tower.

"Nay. I have assembled a search party, but we have found nothing."

She was quiet for several beats. "I fear something terrible has befallen him."

"Do not lose hope yet. We renew our search today."

When they reached the kitchen, Jeremy and Emma were sitting at the table having breakfast.

"Look who decided to wake finally," Jeremy commented.

"A few nights upstairs and she fancies herself a queen," Emma sneered.

"Now that I am well," Miss Daliyah began, "I can return—"

"You will not return to your previous quarters," Addison reminded her. "His lordship has insisted you remain in your present quarters."

Emma and Jeremy looked surprised.

"Is that really necessary?" Emma asked.

"It is," Addison replied. "It were possible her room contained some element that caused her sudden illness. We cannot risk her becoming sick again."

He assembled a plate for Miss Daliyah while Emma told her that Miss Cameron had been quite displeased that she was unavailable for two whole days.

Addison bit his tongue again.

"I will work twice as hard to atone for my absence," Miss Daliyah said.

"You had better," Emma replied. "*I* had to undertake your responsibilities though I had naught to do with your being sick."

"And it was quite benevolent of you to have done so," Addison said to her. "It shows a generosity of spirit."

Emma knit her brows in thought, then smiled in acknowledgment. "I knew all the chores and tasks had to be done. It was quite trying and exhausting for one person to do them all."

"Then you are to be commended."

Her smile broadened.

Hearing Montague ring for him, Addison excused himself. He went upstairs and found Montague sitting at his writing table with his hand over his brow.

"How wise of you to have locked her door last night," Montague said.

Addison drew in a long breath. "You went to her chambers, then."

Montague looked up. "My hunger started returning last night."

"Damnation. But you spent a great deal of time with Miss Cameron yesterday."

"I did, and it was tedious, save when I kissed her."

"Did you feel a difference then?"

"I felt nothing. I intimated that I would

propose to her."

"She was receptive?"

"Aye."

"The sooner you marry her, the better, I think."

Montague slammed his palm on the top of the table. "We've no bloody notion that will suffice. How is the maid?"

"You mean Miss Daliyah? She has made a remarkable recovery."

Montague leaned his head back against his chair and closed his eyes. "You may credit yourself for her being alive. I was interrupted before I could fully feed upon her."

"She seems to have no recollection of what happened, though she said she dreamt of someone coming into her quarters."

"And nothing else?"

"If there is more, she did not reveal it to me. She did note that she was bitten. She can feel the marks upon her neck."

"Tell her it must have been a rat." Montague fisted his hand with a grimace. He released a ragged breath. "The desires are returning in strength."

Addison cursed to himself. "Both of them?"

"As ever, they are intertwined. And I have spent as many hours as possible with Miss Cameron. She fancies herself the Countess of Blackbourne already, for she remarked on how the rooms could be improved."

"Perhaps the consummation of marriage will prove to be the cure."

"Perhaps, but that could be weeks away. In the meantime, I need to address my hunger."

"Can you wait another day?"

"For what purpose? I've no wish to wait another day."

Addison paced the room. "Perhaps you could satiate your appetite with a partial feeding, as you had done with Miss Daliyah."

"What happened with Miss Daliyah was an anomaly. Remember the times you attempted to interrupt my feedings in the hopes of saving the prey? Not a one survived. Once my fangs are in, I want every last drop."

"Then how were you able to stop with Miss Daliyah?"

"I know not. I think I was surprised. I've never spent with such intense euphoria. It was as if…as if I could feel her spending as well. You say she is fully recovered?"

Addison frowned at what the question suggested. "I said she has made a remarkable recovery, given that none of your victims have ever lived to tell about it, but I know not that her full health has returned."

"But sufficient for my purposes."

"What of Emma or Jeremy?"

"And what if I am unable to stop myself? How are we to explain their disappearance? With Miss Daliyah, we can say she ran away. Surely it is not unheard of for indentured servants to run away to escape their servitude."

"She may not survive a second feeding."

Montague cocked a brow. "A tragedy you have witnessed time and again."

Addison rubbed the back of his neck as he continued to pace under Montague's watchful eye.

"As I told you before, you must set aside your fetish for this maid," said Montague. "I think I had best finish her before your feelings of partiality grow."

Addison felt his cheeks warm. "If you could repeat your first feeding with her, would you consider it?"

"You mean your notion of a partial feeding?"

"Yes."

"If it produced the same satisfaction, but we know not that it will."

"We know not that it won't."

"The partial feeding was happenstance because of your presence."

"Then I will have to be present again."

Montague narrowed his eyes at Addison. "You've truly become attached to this girl."

Addison shifted his feet. "There is much goodness in her. I've not met her like."

"If goodness mattered in this world, would I exist as I am?"

Having no response, Addison released a resigned breath.

"Tonight, then," Montague said. "When everyone is asleep, I will have Miss Daliyah, and if you insist upon being present, I will allow it."

Back in his own room, Addison went from feeling relieved that he had convinced Montague to try his strategy to worry that none of it mattered. What if the partial feeding failed? What if he did not interrupt Montague in time? What if it was a near miracle that Miss Daliyah had survived the first feeding and the chances of such fortune occurring again was as likely as lightning striking the same spot twice?

Sitting down on his bed, shoulders slumped, he hung his head. He cursed himself for not having the foresight to go into the village to find another victim for Montague before the appetites returned. He might have spared Miss Daliyah then. Now she would have to suffer a second assault. How could he have been so foolish as to let a few days' reprieve coddle complacency?

He searched his mind for alternatives. Immersed in thought, he did not respond to the knock at his door. It was Emma, no doubt, but he had not the smallest of interest in her company. She persisted in knocking and whispered his name, but he ignored her till she finally relented and went away.

Chapter Nineteen

With Mr. Phillips still absent, Mr. Brooke enlisted Jeremy to assist with the care and grooming of the horses. Jeremy was none too happy to have to take on duties not normally his, though he still had ample time during the day to slumber, toss pebbles into a can, and grouse about his boredom. Daliyah would have liked to care for the horses, for she liked being near the animals. She had often looked with envy upon those who knew how to ride one.

Jeremy came upon her outside where she was washing a stain from one of Miss Cameron's frocks and said, "You've spilt oats all over the stable floor. You had best clean it up."

"But I have not been in the barn stables," Daliyah said.

He narrowed his eyes. "Are you suggesting I spilt it?"

You were the one responsible for feeding the horses today, she wanted to reply. Instead, she remained silent.

"Well, then, what are you waiting for?" he demanded.

"I have garments of Miss Cameron's to wash," she said.

"Then make sure you attend to the mess in the stables when you are done."

"When she is done," said Mr. Brooke, who had come upon them unnoticed, "I have need of her services. I would be much obliged if you took care of the stables, Jeremy."

Jeremy could not look more displeased, but Mr. Brooke stared him down. Grumbling beneath his breath, Jeremy headed to the stables. When he was gone, Mr. Brooke turned to Daliyah.

"Do you ever tell him or Emma to leave off?" he asked.

She returned to scrubbing the frock. "There is not to be gained save their ire."

"But you have thought it, surely?"

She hid her smile, then looked up at Mr. Brooke, who grinned.

"I would be much worried had you never had such a thought," he said. "I've a mind to wring their necks, and I am but a witness of their treatment toward you."

"On that matter, I fear your kindness towards me has made them jealous."

Emma, in particular, had grown more antagonistic. She had willfully brushed past Daliyah, bumping her into the entry of the kitchen. She had also knocked over a plate of apple slices Daliyah had prepared for herself, though she claimed it to be an accident.

"They ought not be permitted such childish behavior," Mr. Brooke said, "and childish be an overly benign term for how they act. You do not deserve to suffer their oppression."

"I have come to accept what comes my way. Far worse could befall me."

His features darkened, and he looked away. "Have you never brought their atrocious behavior to the attentions of your master?"

"When I was in Barbados, I saw the young son of the overseer steal a slingshot a slave boy

204

had made for himself. When he asked for its return, he received twenty lashes upon his back."

Mr. Brooke was silent.

"If you wish to improve their sentiments towards me," she continued, "I urge you not to be so kind to me."

His gaze remained elsewhere, and a muscle along his jaw rippled. "I could not treat you as they do."

"You could be indifferent."

He looked at her and seemed almost sorrowful. "If that is what you wish."

She nodded. He continued to frown.

"Your restraint is greater than mine," he said, looking away again.

She studied him and sensed he had his own troubles to bear. She inquired gently, "Is it?"

He looked at her. Something inside him called to her. Was it helplessness? Pain? His mouth opened, but no words emerged. Abruptly, he turned on his heels and strode away.

*****

"It is only fair that you provide Emma some

relief as she has had to take on your duties during your illness," Miss Cameron said while sitting at the vanity and studying her complexion before the looking glass.

"Yes, mistress," Daliyah replied as she removed the bedpans.

"I will look my best tomorrow. A countess must always look her best. She is a reflection of her husband, and I mean to make Lord Blackbourne proud. Once he sees how I can bring him admiration, he will surely want to venture more into society. He is exceptionally amiable. It makes no sense why he hides away in this old castle."

An involuntary shiver went through Daliyah.

Leaning in toward the looking glass, Miss Cameron smoothed her brows. "What think you of my being the Countess of Blackbourne?"

"You would make a beautiful countess, mistress," Daliyah replied as she stood by with Miss Cameron's nightcap.

"I think I will wear my marigold taffeta gown tomorrow. I like the low décolletage."

"Very good," Daliyah said as she fitted the cap over Miss Cameron's locks, which caught the glow of the candlelight.

"I pray that you will be more careful. It is distressing enough to have Mr. Phillips gone, but if you were to fall ill a second time, it would be more than an inconvenience. You have truly trespassed upon Lord Blackbourne's hospitality beyond reason. That he insists you spend another night in superior chambers shows the depth of his munificence and likely his desire to earn my good graces. It is far more than you deserve."

After Daliyah assisted Miss Cameron into bed and snuffed the candles, she went upstairs to prepare her own bed. While the chambers were beyond sumptuous to her, she did not like its placement so far from the others. She wished Mr. Brooke had been able to convince Lord Blackbourne to let her return to the servants' quarters.

In the chambers, she found a fire burning in the hearth and a bedpan beneath the bedclothes. The work of Mr. Brooke, no doubt.

Setting down her candle, she began to disrobe down to her chemise. After removing the bedpan, she slid into bed, marveling at its warmth. Dear Mr. Brooke! Why was he so kind to her? Perhaps he pitied her. But that did not disturb her. She found him a lovely person and could not help but feel a little in love with him for all his kindness.

In her mind, she relived the moment he had held her hand, when only inches had separated them. She had wanted him to kiss her, but she knew he would not. Though his interest in her was palpable, he knew better than to choose her when he could have the likes of Miss Emma. Nevertheless, Daliyah relished the moments she shared with Mr. Brooke and drifted to sleep with thoughts of him.

She woke when the fire had dwindled to embers. Looking at the door, she wondered if it was locked. She wished it were. A locked door trapped her in the room, but it could prevent an intruder from entering. Lest they had a key.

Of a sudden, every nerve in her body was awake. The footsteps from the prior night had returned.

Chapter Twenty

The poker!

She should have set the fireplace utensil beside her bed earlier. Throwing back the covers, Daliyah slid out of bed and reached the poker just as the chamber door opened.

"Who goes there?" she asked as malevolence filled the air.

The silhouette of a man approached in slow and measured steps. The shadow from her dreams! Her grip tightened upon the poker. As he came closer, she saw the angles of his physiognomy, faintly illuminated by the embers of the fire.

"Lord Blackbourne?"

"Forgive me, *ma enfant*," he said before

easily ripping the poker from her grasp.

She backed away.

"How m-may I assist you, my lord?" she stammered, attempting to keep the distance between them as he continued stepping forward.

"You need only submit," he replied.

Her heartbeat went wild. He kept advancing and would eventually back her into the wall behind her. She attempted to sprint around him, but he caught her by the waist and threw her toward the bed. She scrambled back to her feet and tried to run again, but he was upon her, a heavy and familiar weight.

She pushed and hit at him, but her strikes glanced off him without effect as if he were made of stone. He grabbed her wrists and pinned them above her head. Her body rounded the edge of the bed, and she attempted to slide down, but she was trapped beneath him. She kicked and twisted, all to no avail.

"My lord, please," she pleaded as he lowered his head.

She thought he intended to kiss her on the mouth.

Instead, he went for her neck.

She cried out when she felt the pierce of his teeth. How were they so sharp? She struggled harder, though she was no match for his strength.

Just as in her dream—what she had thought a dream—she felt herself bleeding, felt his mouth upon her, sucking. And then warmth spread from where he had seared her neck. It settled in her loins, and she found herself yearning for him. Her body had ceased its struggles and failed to resist when he nudged her legs apart with his knee. She heard herself moan.

He released her wrists to pull up her chemise, which she welcomed and invited by pressing her hips against his. With a growl, he unbuttoned his fall and pulled out his hardened member. He speared into her eager cunnie, already wet for his entry. The warmth in her body collapsed into a poignant yearning between her legs. He pushed himself farther into her. Wanting more, she ground herself onto his erection, grunting and gasping as he filled her deeper and deeper.

With every thrust, her ardor grew. She needed release, but he found his first. With a feral roar, he quickened the motions of his hips before coming to a stop. His legs trembled. He stabbed into her a few more times before he exhaled and lowered his head toward her neck again.

"Enough," another voice commanded.

Turning her head, she saw that they were not alone.

Chapter Twenty - One

It sickened and aroused Addison to see Miss Daliyah pinned beneath his brother, halfway upon the bed, her chemise drawn up, exposing her bare legs, spread with Montague between them.

Blood churned in his groin. It had been no easy matter, witnessing Montague ravishing Miss Daliyah. He had wanted to look away several times, but he needed to keep a watchful eye to ensure that Montague did not drink too much of her blood. He prayed that she would survive, as she had done the first time.

"Mr. Brooke?" she murmured as she stared at him through glazed eyes.

He groaned to hear his name. He wanted to

be anywhere but here, and yet, with the room filled with the scent of lust, he could not move, rooted by his own penetrating desires.

Montague stirred, and Addison decided it was best he remove him should his thirst for blood overcome him. He walked over just as Montague withdrew and rolled onto his back, collapsing on the bed beside Miss Daliyah. Addison reached for Montague to pull him away, but he was stayed by Miss Daliyah, who placed a hand upon his forearm. Sitting up on the bed, she grabbed his other arm. He saw ardor swimming in her eyes, and for a moment he fancied that she desired him, but he knew the sentiment had been placed there by Montague's feeding.

"Miss Daliyah—" he choked.

She pulled him toward her.

"You must not," he groaned. Every nerve in his body wanted him to relent, but he ought not take advantage of her condition.

When he refused to move closer, she shifted to her knees upon the bed. She tugged at his cravat till it came loose, then kissed his throat.

Bloody hell.

Silently, he cursed Montague a dozen times

even as he savored the sensation of her soft, full lips against his skin. She kissed her way to his jaw, and his resistance began to crumble.

"Miss Daliyah, please desist," he whispered as heat throbbed in his loins. "Desist—"

She smothered his words with her lips.

Glory bloomed in his defeat. Cupping her face in his hands, he returned her kiss, harder and deeper. By God, she did taste sweet, as Montague had said. He tasted of her mouth and all its parts: the lips, the tongue, and even the teeth. If it were not for the urgency boiling in his cods, he would have been content to kiss her forever.

She, too, seemed impatient, for she fell back to the bed, pulling him with her. He landed atop her. His head swirled at the feel of her curves beneath him, her legs bumping into his. She grabbed his head and kissed him ferociously. His cock stretched against his breeches as she started undulating her hips.

A small voice persisted in telling him that what he did was wrong, but his ardor spoke louder.

When she reached for the buttons of his fall, he pulled aside her chemise. She freed his cock and placed its tip at her slit. Desire spun through him, and this time, he cursed *himself.*

This was not how he would've chosen to bed Miss Daliyah, but her desire was too intoxicating. Every aspect—the scent of her, the sight of her eyes bright with lust, the softness of her bosom, the smoothness of her legs as they brushed against him, all beckoned, all inflamed his own desire.

He kissed her gently upon the neck, tasting the blood Montague had left. She wrapped her arms around his neck and pulled his mouth once more toward hers. He had never before kissed such thick and supple lips, and he found them divine. Their tongues brushed. He understood how Montague could want more of this, how he might drain her without intention because she was that delicious.

Addison wanted to worship more of her, but she seemed impatient, angling her hips to sheath herself upon his cock. Obliging, he sank into her wet heat. It mattered not that the wetness owed itself in part to Montague's mettle, for she felt utterly magnificent. The blissful embrace of her cunnie about his pulsing shaft seemed to spread through his body, to his head and to every extremity. When he gazed into her eyes and looked upon her parted lips, he thought he felt her euphoria as well, as if in joining their bodies, they had become one.

She rocked her hips at him, a signal to begin the dance. Casting aside the final whispers of his conscience, he thrust in earnest. Her gasps were a heady symphony filling his ears. He wanted nothing more than to hear her cries of rapture.

Tempering his own need for release, he thrust at a pace and angle that made her smile as her lashes fluttered. She urged him on with quickened groans, her grasp upon his arms tightening. Then, for several seconds, she became silent before her body started to shudder, her cunnie spasmed about his cock, and she released her cry of ecstasy.

Her climax swelled within him, sending him over the edge. With several ferocious pumps of the hips, he emptied himself into her in the most incredible ecstasy his body had ever known.

He remained inside her, his cock pulsing, his heart beating rapidly, erratic tremors shaking his legs.

When he surfaced from the whirlpool of

carnal bliss, his conscience returned with a vengeance.

He knew then he was damned.

Chapter Twenty - Two

While basking in the bliss of his carnal release, Montague idly watched as Addison sank himself into Daliyah, his shaky groan an indication of the pleasure he felt. Montague knew the heaven Addison was in. He could recall it all: her warmth, her wetness, the ripple of her cunnie as it embraced his cock. He watched Daliyah's brow furrow, heard her moans, smelled her desire. Her rutting and writhing in lust was the most titillating sight.

Arousal warmed his loins once more, but it was the muted passions of a man and not the tortured cravings of a monster.

He watched as she cried out and shuddered.

Her pleasure had boiled over into spasms. He became jealous of Addison for being the one to vault her to her climax. He would have liked to have been the one to cause her to shake so.

Yet he was glad when Addison spent, glad that his brother had had a turn. He suspected Addison had been none too pleased to have to stand and watch him ravish Miss Daliyah if he could not also partake of her.

Montague contemplated a second helping of the maid, but Addison might object. Deciding not to disturb the pair, he rose from the bed to return to his own chambers.

The following morning, he woke with the same satiation he had felt the morning after his first feeding with Miss Daliyah. He rang for Addison, who did not look as refreshed as Montague felt.

"You appear rather glum," Montague commented. "Was Miss Daliyah's cunnie not to your satisfaction?"

He regretted his words when Addison shot him a hard look.

"How does she fare?" Montague asked.

"She sleeps."

Standing over the basin, Montague washed

220

his face. "She is alive, then."

Addison nodded. "I sat by her side the rest of the night."

Little wonder he looked weary.

Addison continued, "She was not as cold to the touch as the first time. I take it you drank less of her blood last night."

"In truth, I think I fed as much last night as I had the first."

"And do you feel full? Are your appetites gone?"

"They are. I think it no coincidence that I have felt satiated both times that I have fed upon her," Montague said as he sat down for his shave. "Her blood is special. I wonder what would happen if I fed upon her fully?"

Addison, who was sharpening the razor blade, stopped. "And if it did nothing? You would have killed the only victim to have given you relief from your hunger."

"True. I gather I should not chance it."

"What of Miss Cameron?"

"At present, she appears quite useless."

"But she is the nearest solution we have."

"It were still possible that the witch's final words are all a lie, a farce to toy with my hopes."

Addison applied the shaving cream. "But you still intend to marry Miss Cameron. We must retain her, should she prove to be the solution we seek."

Montague nodded. He would wed Miss Cameron, ravish her, and feed upon her. If, after all that, he was still not cured, then perhaps hope never truly existed for him.

Addison passed the blade along Montague's jaw. "Today the search party will make a last effort to find Mr. Phillips. If you wish, I can tell Miss Cameron that it will take another day or two to find a new driver and set of horses."

Montague thought for a moment. Miss Cameron grew less enchanting the more he knew her. She had few interests beyond fashion and gossip. Though she was not dull of wit, her commentaries revolved around matters he found mundane.

"That is unnecessary," he decided. "Lengthening her stay serves no purpose and will only spur speculation. It is better she were on her way."

"Are you certain?"

"Engage the driver and horses today so that she may depart on the morrow."

Addison was quiet for several minutes before finally asking, "What of Miss Daliyah?"

"She will remain here, of course. I have need of her."

Addison made no response.

"Are you not pleased?" Montague asked. "You seem to favor her company and her cunnie."

Addison flushed. "I would not—had she—that is…"

Montague smirked. "You're welcome."

Addison threw the razor down with anger. "The circumstances were hardly what I would have wished!"

"Nevertheless, you availed yourself of the opportunity my intervention provided."

Addison turned away and braced himself against the sideboard. "I was too weak to withstand my desires."

"You are merely human," Montague consoled.

"A poor excuse."

"You did what every other man would have done."

Addison shook his head. Done with the shave, Montague removed the linen from about his neck and stood. It was a shame Addison's mother had raised him with more morals than their father had. It led only to more pain for his brother.

"Such is life," Montague said, "its inequities, senselessness, and misery. One can strive for goodness, but in the end, there are no rewards. You are a better man than I, yet we are both cursed the same."

With only a sigh, Addison put away the shaving articles, then went to assist Montague with his wardrobe.

While tying Montague's cravat, Addison asked, "What are we to tell Miss Daliyah when she wakes?"

"Did you lock her door?"

"I did."

"Then we need not tell her anything."

Montague noted Addison's frown and said, "I will tell Miss Cameron that her maid has taken ill again and offer my home till she recovers."

"Miss Daliyah will ask why we are holding her prisoner."

"Tell her she is a guest at Blackbourne."

"She is no fool."

Montague scowled. "Tell her whatever you

bloody wish, then."

Once dressed, Montague dismissed Addison, not wanting his brother's sullen mood to taint his own more sanguine disposition. No hunger gnawed at him the whole of the day, and he tolerated the company of Miss Cameron in even better spirits than the days before. While they walked the grounds, he listened with half an ear to her prattle on about who was likely to marry whom this Season and how astonished everyone was that the very plain daughter of a baronet had managed to snatch a viscount. As they walked, he took in the shape of the clouds and even the sound of the birds. When he grew bored, he flirted with Miss Cameron.

"If the search party is unable to find Mr. Phillips, I will have Addison engage another driver and team of horses," he told her, "though I must admit, selfishly, that you could extend your stay."

They stood in the gazebo of his garden. Miss Cameron leaned against a column, looking away, idly fanning herself.

She turned to him. "You have been such a gracious host, I find I am in no hurry to leave."

He stepped toward her and braced an arm

against the column. "You will write to me when you arrive in London?"

"Of course. Every day, if you wish."

"I do indeed."

"And you will come to London?"

Gently, he lifted her chin. "I shall indeed."

She closed her eyes, likely expecting to be kissed. With a smile to himself, he obliged and pressed his lips to hers. She did not return in kind but stayed as she was while he dictated the kiss. When he parted from her, she released a soft sigh. Her eyes glimmered.

"London will be quite dreary without you," she said.

"And Blackbourne will return to its prior gloom without your bright presence," he lied.

He would be relieved not to have to feign interest in Miss Cameron. And while their kiss had not been unpleasant, it was tedious compared to the warmth that flared within him when he had taken Miss Daliyah's lips. The splendor of their congress astonished him still. And if he could stall his appetites by feeding upon and ravishing Miss Daliyah, he might have little need for Miss Cameron. It remained uncertain that Miss Cameron could cure him—

if a cure even existed.

He offered Miss Cameron his arm as they returned to the castle, no longer circled by rain clouds. The sun shone unhindered. Montague rarely found himself grateful, but on this day, he felt as if Fortune had finally deigned to smile upon him. For the time being, as long as he had Miss Daliyah, he had hope for better days, hope that he could have some semblance of man over beast.

Printed in Great Britain
by Amazon